LIONBOY
THE TRUTH

Praise for the *Lionboy, Lionboy: The Chase* and *Lionboy: The Truth*:

'A new star has appeared in the children's literary firmament' – *Independent*

'Simply absolutely brilliant' – *Disney's Big Time*

'A cracking pace and excellent jokes' – *Guardian*

'Vivid and engaging' – *The Times*

'One of the best books of the year' – *Mail on Sunday*

'The itch to know what happens next is strong' – *Daily Telegraph*

'Stunning' – *Daily Express*

'Fabulous' – *Observer*

'Thrilling moments and dangerous scrapes . . . We give this read a big paws up!' – *Funday Times*

'An evocative, suspenseful tale of betrayal and courage' – *Sunday Times*

'Sparkling in wit and fantasy' – *TES*

Books by Zizou Corder

LIONBOY

LIONBOY: THE CHASE

LIONBOY: THE TRUTH

LIONBOY
THE TRUTH

ZIZOU CORDER

PUFFIN BOOKS

Published by the Penguin Group
Penguin Books Ltd, 80 Strand, London WC2R ORL, England
Penguin Group (USA) Inc., 375 Hudson Street, New York, New York 10014, USA
Penguin Group (Canada), 90 Eglinton Avenue East, Suite 700, Toronto, Ontario, Canada M4P 2Y3
(a division of Pearson Penguin Canada Inc.)
Penguin Ireland, 25 St Stephen's Green, Dublin 2, Ireland (a division of Penguin Books Ltd)
Penguin Group (Australia), 250 Camberwell Road, Camberwell, Victoria 3124, Australia
(a division of Pearson Australia Group Pty Ltd)
Penguin Books India Pvt Ltd, 11 Community Centre, Panchsheel Park, New Delhi – 110 017, India
Penguin Group (NZ), 67 Apollo Drive, Mairangi Bay, Auckland 1310, New Zealand
(a division of Pearson New Zealand Ltd)
Penguin Books (South Africa) (Pty) Ltd, 24 Sturdee Avenue, Rosebank, Johannesburg 2196, South Africa

Penguin Books Ltd, Registered Offices: 80 Strand, London WC2R ORL, England

penguin.com

First published 2006
Published in this edition 2007
1

Text copyright © Zizou Corder, 2006
Illustrations copyright © Fred van Deelen, 2006
Music copyright © Robert Lockhart, 2006
All rights reserved

The moral right of the author and illustrator has been asserted

Set in Perpetua
Typeset by Palimpsest Book Production Limited, Grangemouth, Stirlingshire
Made and printed in England by Clays Ltd, St Ives plc

British Library Cataloguing in Publication Data
A CIP catalogue record for this book is available from the British Library

ISBN: 978-0-141-31757-1

To Jack and Ralph Jeffries,
top boys

ACKNOWLEDGEMENTS

Thanks yet again to the usual honorees: Fred van Deelen for his beautiful maps and diagrams, and to Paul Hodgson for presenting the music to match.

The lovely Puffin ladies, with their everlastingly lovely footwear, specially Sarah Hughes, Adele Minchin, Tania Vian-Smith, Kirsten Grant, Elaine McQuade, Lesley Levene, Shannon Park and Francesca Dow. And the Puffin gentlemen, Tom Sanderson, for our glamorous and dramatic new cover look, and Matt Phillips.

And the agents: Linda Shaughnessy, Rob Kraitt, Teresa Nicholls, Anjali Pratap, Sylvie Rabineau. And Derek Johns: is he totally without flaw?

And to Melanie Phillips for helping design San Antonio.

Special thanks again to Robert Lockhart for writing us a gorgeous evocative soundtrack. Most of the tunes are available in a book written for the piano, with a CD of the music played by a small orchestra, so you don't even have to play it yourself. It is called
Music from Zizou Corder's **Lionboy**,
*by Robert Lockhart, and published by
Faber Music. You can get it from music shops
or online from www.fabermusic.com.*

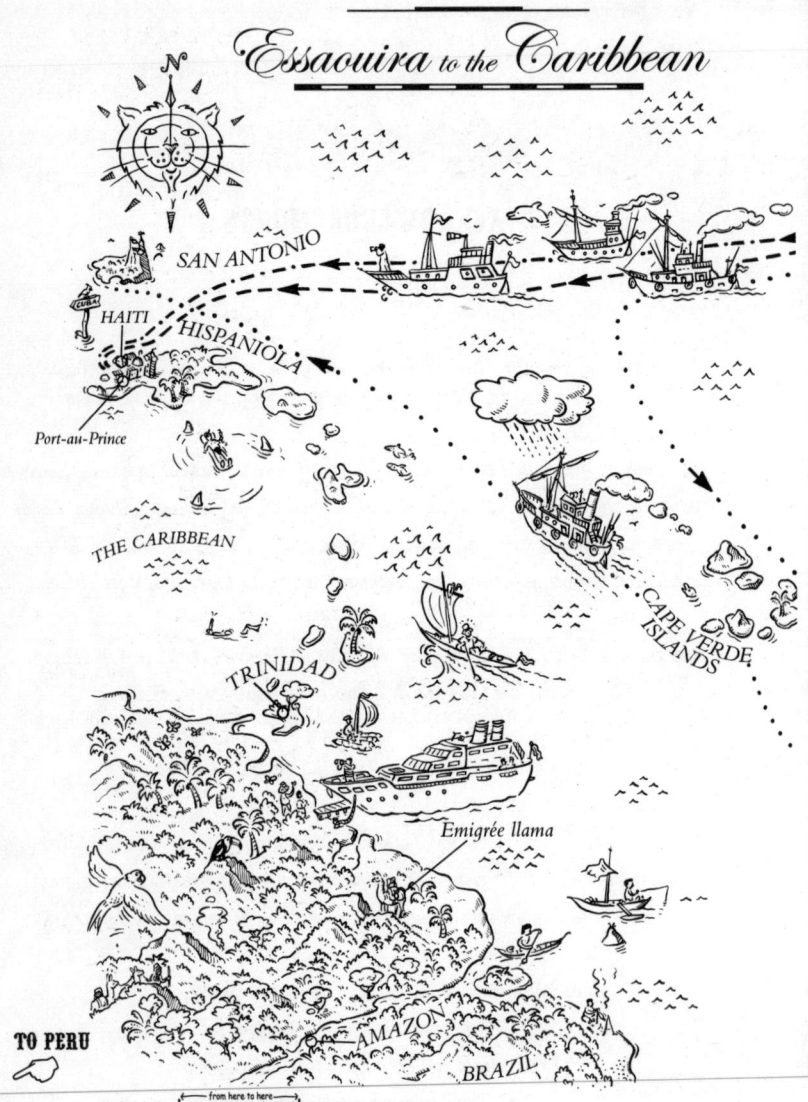

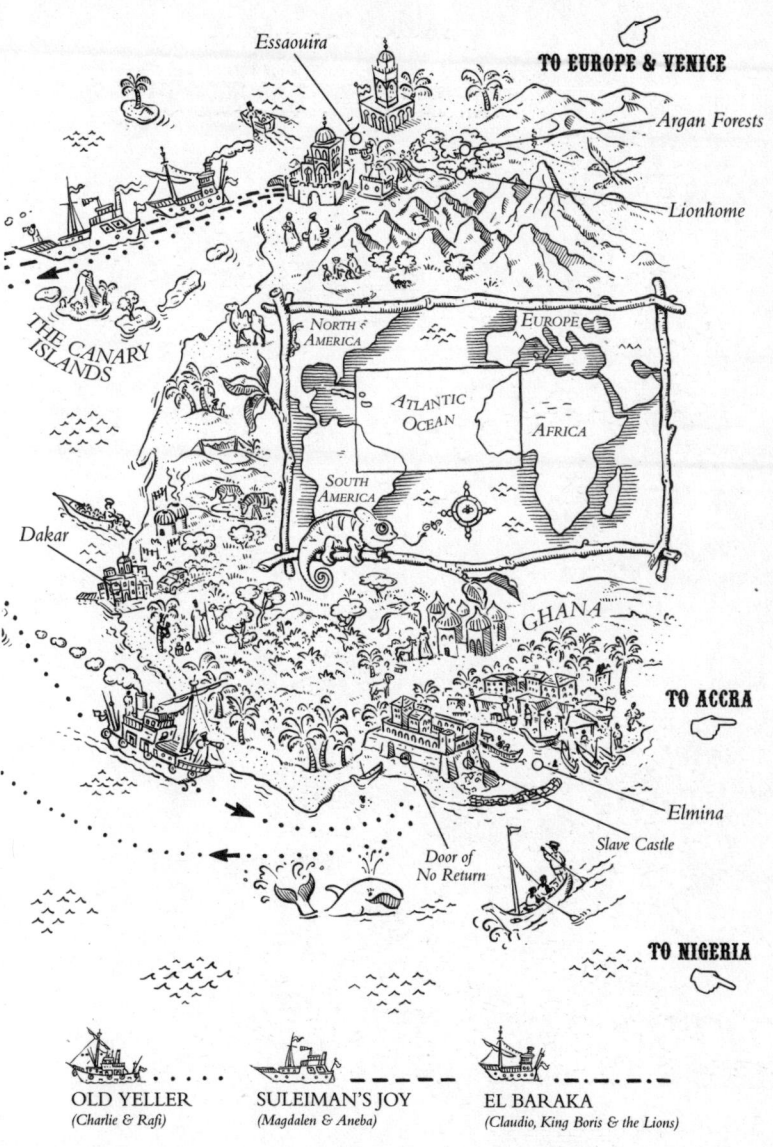

Essaouira

TO EUROPE & VENICE

Argan Forests

Lionhome

THE CANARY ISLANDS

NORTH AMERICA

ATLANTIC OCEAN

EUROPE

AFRICA

SOUTH AMERICA

Dakar

GHANA

TO ACCRA

Elmina

Slave Castle

Door of No Return

TO NIGERIA

OLD YELLER
(Charlie & Rafi)

SULEIMAN'S JOY
(Magdalen & Aneba)

EL BARAKA
(Claudio, King Boris & the Lions)

CHAPTER
ONE

In a cool high room in a hot, hot country, a sleeping boy wriggled and twitched his nose. Charlie Ashanti, Lion-rescuer, shipwreck-survivor, Circus veteran, son of asthma-cure-inventing scientists and Catspeaker, had been asleep for three days – out of sheer relief. He had, in recent months, been chased across Europe, delivered six escaped circus Lions back to their African home, rescued a cloned prehistoric creature, assisted in a revolution, punched his enemy and watched him run away and, finally, found the kidnapped parents for whom he had been desperately searching. In other words, he was a very happy boy, just beginning to stir and stretch in his bed after a most well-deserved and refreshing rest.

And as he stretched, he realized that his feet were far nearer the end of the bed. They used to sort of float about halfway down and not touch the end unless he wriggled down that far on purpose. He'd grown. He was delighted.

'Mum!' he called. 'I can reach the end of my bed!'

Charlie and his parents had reunited, after all their adventures, at a particularly beautiful hotel called the Riad el Amira, in the town of Essaouira on the Barbary Coast of Morocco. It was now about six in the morning, and Charlie had been woken by a light finger of low, early sunshine on his face.

'Mum!' he called again.

From the other bed came the unmistakable snuffly sound of a mother who is fast asleep and not prepared to wake up for any lesser reason than the house being on fire, in which case she'll see what she can do. Dad was snoring. The whole place, actually, was vibrating gently with the strength of it.

'I need measuring!' he called. 'I've grown!'

'*Bnnffmmmmffffbbbrrr*,' said his mum.

Typical, thought Charlie. We haven't seen each other for months, we've been through all this stuff, and now they just want to sleep. Hmph. (Having been asleep, he didn't know that they had been checking on him regularly and affectionately, longing for him to wake and tell them his adventures, but unable to be so mean as to wake him.)

Charlie got up anyway, and went over to look at his parents asleep in bed. How sweet they looked, all snuggled up. Magdalen and Aneba, heads on the pillow. He smiled at them. They had been through a lot too.

Plenty of time, he thought cheerfully, deciding not to

wake them. Instead he got dressed – someone had laid out for him a new pair of britches and a T-shirt – and, as it was chilly, he slipped into the battered circus jacket that he'd been wearing ever since the night he and the Lions had run off. The gold braid was salt-tarnished and half the buttons were missing, and he liked it very much. He and it had been through stuff together.

He went down to the hotel's deserted courtyard. He was starving. Also he wanted to find Sergei, his mangy Allergenie cat friend, who, though he was not half as evil as he looked, looked so evil that he had been banned from the hotel. Charlie hadn't had a chance to see him for – well, how long had he been asleep? Must be days. They would have to go to a café for breakfast. Charlie wanted to go to the one where the chameleon had spoken to him in Cat.

Sergei was outside in the narrow alley, scratching himself on the corner of the building. He looked as if he'd been up all night. In a bar. With villains. His black fur was lank on his skinny body, his ear was wonky (though that was Charlie's fault – he'd fixed it on badly in Venice, after Sergei had lost it in a fight) and his tail looked even balder than usual in the early morning sunlight.

'Hey, Sergei!' cried Charlie.

'Monsieur awakes!' Sergei responded in his cheerful yet sarcastic North of England voice. 'How are yer then, Sleepin' Beauty? Had yer kip? Feelin' all right? How are your esteemed parents? All in one piece, are they? Thanks for takin' the trouble to keep me up to date, as it were, on the developments within this illustrious establishment wherefrom I am *banned*. Not that I've been prowling pathetically around the joint yearning to partake of your bulletins. Obviously, having just traversed Europe by boat with you and your band of ex-performing felines, the last thing I need is to be told what's goin' on . . .'

'Stop moaning, Sergei,' said Charlie, giving him an affectionate ruffle on his skinny, scarred head. 'Nothing's been going on. I've been asleep, my parents are fine.' Here he gave a big grin. His parents were fine! He was fine! The Lions were home, Sergei was here, Rafi Sadler had scarpered with his tail between his legs – as it were. Of course, Rafi didn't actually have a tail. Yes, everything was fine!

'Well, I'm glad to hear it,' said Sergei, and he was because, although he affected a grumpy and sarcastic manner, Sergei was a loyal, true and brilliant cat. 'What's for breakfast then?'

'Omelettes, pastries, mangoes, chocolate croissants, cakes, honey, pitta bread, argan oil, more mangoes, yog-hurt . . .' said Charlie hungrily.

'Fish heads,' said Sergei firmly. 'I'll just nip down the harbour and pick something up. See you at the caff in a minute.'

*

Magdalen was still snuffling slee[...] Charlie had been talking to her.

She rolled over and looked ac[...] 'Charlie? Oh my god, where is he?'

She hurtled out of bed, Aneba called[...] five minutes she was at the café, where [...] in conversation with a small green chamele[...] [s]at in a creeper on the terrace, talking about wh[y] on earth a chameleon would be able to speak Cat. 'I am *very* chameleon,' the creature, whose name was Ninu, was saying. 'Not just colour but everything!'

'Charlie,' said Magdalen, her red hair all mussed and her shirt on funny. She looked like she'd just got out of bed (which, of course, she had). She didn't notice her son's tiny companion.

Charlie leapt up and flung his arms round her. 'Hi, Mum!' he said. His smile felt too big for his face. She wrapped her arms round him too and held very tight.

'We must get back to the hotel,' she said. 'It's not safe to be running around. Come on.'

Charlie squinted up at her.

'Enemies, Charlie?' she said quietly, pulling him into the shadows. 'Rafi? The Corporacy? I know we've seen them off for the moment, but they do all still exist. Come on . . .'

Put that way, he saw what she meant. Rafi *could* still be here. Perhaps a café terrace on the main square was not the

. . . for Charlie to be, even if it was only just after . . . . . ise.

'Yeah,' he mumbled. 'Sorry.'

He gave Ninu a longing look. The chameleon seemed to grin at him with his long, wide mouth. He had a frill round the back of his neck and googly eyes that went in different directions independently.

'Come on,' said Magdalen, taking Charlie's arm and giving the waiter, who had come out to take Charlie's order, an apologetic look. She knew what these small towns were like. Everybody noticed everything.

'Charlie,' she said as soon as they were safely on a side street, heading back for the hotel. 'We've *got* to be careful. All of us.'

At that moment scrofulent Sergei reappeared by Charlie's shin. 'All right, don't wait for me then,' he complained. 'Ignore me for three days, come out to breakfast with me and then stand me up, why don't you?'

'Oh, do be quiet, Sergei,' said Charlie affectionately.

Magdalen looked down. Of course she knew Charlie talked to cats, but she never got used to it.

'Um . . . hello, Sergei,' said Magdalen. 'Wow.' She smiled at him. Sergei had found her and Aneba in the Corporacy Community to which they had been taken when they were kidnapped. He had led them out – rescued them. She wondered how to address him. Charlie had told her that cats could usually understand human, but even so . . . 'Wow,' she said again.

'Mraow,' said Sergei, flicking his whiskers. It sounded very like 'wow'. Magdalen smiled.

Back at the hotel, Aneba folded Charlie in his huge arms. He felt his son's strong heartbeat, and noticed his added height and bigger shoulders.

'Hello, boy,' he said. 'Nice to see you up, but please could you manage to stick around and not immediately disappear again? Now that we have you back?'

Breakfast was waiting for them in the courtyard.

'Coffee,' said Magdalen.

'And explanations,' said Aneba, giving his son a smile the size of a house.

There was so much to tell. Charlie went first, all in a rush as his parents' jaws dropped.

'Well,' he said. 'Rafi Sadler stole me, and so I escaped and I came after you because you'd disappeared, and I ended up on the *Circe*, this circus boat going to Paris, and I made friends with the Lions, who were being drugged by this evil Liontrainer guy called Maccomo, and I helped them to run away and we all got on a train to Venice, because that's where I thought you were, and we met the King of Bulgaria and went to stay in his palazzo, only his guy Edward got a bit funny and gave us – me and the Lions – to the Doge, who's like the King of Venice, so we had to run away again, and the gondoliers helped us because they were trying to get rid of the Doge anyway, and Sergei – you know Sergei – yeah, well, him – he turned up again from Paris, and Primo – the sabre-toothed extinct Lion, we met him in Paris too, he'd been cloned from a fossil – Edward gave him artificial wings so all the Venetians thought he was St Mark's Lion and he's still there, with Claudio, he's the gondolier, and he got us the solarboat and we came here in it, only we were shipwrecked, and Maccomo and Rafi were after us, but I found out about the Allergenies and how you were kidnapped because of inventing the asthma cure . . .'

Magdalen was staring in amazement. 'You *what?*' she said. 'Slow down.'

Aneba was more precise. 'How did you find out about the Allergenies?' he asked.

'Don't know,' said Charlie. 'Worked it out – somehow some cats were much more allergenic than others, and making all the children asthmatic again, and the cats were all fighting between themselves because cats were being turned out of their homes, because people couldn't afford the medicine for their kids – then it turned out Sergei was one . . . But what happened to *you?*'

'Rafi tricked us,' said Magdalen, looking a bit embarrassed. 'We were carted off on the submarine, then on a truck. We were brought to . . . Do you know about the Corporacy, Charlie?'

'Of course,' said Charlie. 'They're the ones who tried to stop you using your asthma cure. They had Rafi kidnap you.'

'How do you know that?' said Aneba, amazed.

'Cats told me,' said Charlie.

'Do the cats know?' said Magdalen eagerly. 'Do they know all about it?'

'Of course,' said Charlie, wondering how his parents could be so dim. 'They know about the Allergenies being created, genetically modified, to make the kids asthmatic again, because there aren't any cars any more to make them asthmatic, and they know about you and the cure – you're heroes! They think you're fantastic!'

At this point, a beautiful red-haired woman appeared behind his mother.

'Good morning, Mabel,' said Aneba. 'Did you sleep well? Look, Charlie's awake at last!'

At the sight of the woman, Charlie was more than awake. He was in shock.

'What the –!' cried Charlie. 'What –! What's she doing here?'

'Cats told you?' Mabel said. '*Cats* told you?' Her eyes were gleaming and she'd fixed him with her stare.

Charlie stared back. He was completely confused.

'Charlie,' said Magdalen. 'This is your Aunt Mabel.'

Charlie blinked. *Aunt* Mabel? She wasn't an aunt – she was Mabel Stark, world-famous tiger trainer, and Maccomo's kind-of girlfriend.

'She's my sister,' said Magdalen. She watched Charlie carefully, noticing how he took the news.

Charlie blinked again.

'Can you really talk to them?' Mabel was asking.

'Do sit down, Mabel,' said Magdalen. 'He's had a shock. Do you want some coffee?'

Charlie was having a big problem adjusting to this development. Last time he'd seen this woman, she had been hanging out in a very friendly fashion with his two great enemies, Maccomo and Rafi. How come she was suddenly here – and his aunt? How come his mother was offering her coffee, and he was evidently to have breakfast with her? And he wished she'd stop staring at him like that. He shot his mother a pleading glance.

'Mabel!' said Magdalen. 'Get a grip. Coffee? And give him a break.'

The spell that seemed to have been holding Mabel snapped.

'Oh – oh yes, please,' she said. 'Black. Thank you.' She pulled a chair up to their table and sat between Magdalen and Aneba.

'You can tell her,' said Magdalen. 'It's all right.'

Charlie didn't usually tell people about his special gift. He had always known that it was not something to show off about. But if Mum said it was all right, and if Mabel was his aunt . . . even if she did use to be Maccomo's girlfriend . . .

'I *can* talk to them,' he said.

Mabel's green eyes flashed a little wider. Maccomo had told her Charlie was a Catspeaker, but she had hardly dared to believe it.

'Tell me about it,' Mabel said intently. 'How did it come about?'

Even as she said it, Charlie realized something. She was jealous – like Maccomo had been when he had realized. It made Charlie feel strong – grown-ups envying him. It also made him feel nervous. If they wanted what he had, might they try to get it off him?

'I was scratched by a baby leopard when I was little, in Ghana,' he said. 'Some kind of freak genetic exchange happened, with his blood and mine. Don't know why.'

'Can you talk to tigers?' asked Mabel greedily.

Charlie suddenly tired of her questions. He wanted to say, 'Back off!' but he was too polite. Instead he burst out, 'Well, how come you're my aunt? You never used to be my aunt.'

Though, come to think of it, she did look like Magdalen: red hair and ice-white skin. Charlie hadn't noticed it before, when he'd seen her at the Circus with Maccomo. He'd just thought she was beautiful, with her laugh, and her famous tiger act, and her white leather catsuit.

'I –' said Mabel, and then stopped. Magdalen was watching closely to see how she'd put it. 'I – I ran away from home, Charlie, when I was very young, to join the

Circus. I ran away and never told anyone where I'd gone, and the first time I saw anyone from my family was when Magdalen turned up on the *Circe*, looking for you.'

Now it was Charlie's moment for amazement.

'Crike,' he said. 'Why did you do that? Was Grandma horrible? I always thought she was really nice – she was nice to me . . .'

Mabel was making funny little movements with her mouth. She looked upset. Aneba touched her knee kindly. Magdalen was very still, looking at Mabel.

Charlie, looking at the grown-ups, could not make sense of the feelings going on between them. To be honest, it rather embarrassed him that they were having feelings at all.

'Yeah, well,' he said, wanting to change the subject and put them out of their misery. And also wanting to know what had happened to his parents – apart from acquiring this unlikely aunt for him. 'So, Dad, where *did* the Corporacy take you? I know it was near Vence, because someone got it wrong and sent me to Venice instead . . .'

'We were in one of their Gated Communities,' said Aneba, 'and they were brainwashing us like they do everybody they get their hands on, telling us how marvellous everything was, and then your friend Sergei turned up. He saved us. He woke me up with a great scratch across my face, and led us through the smelliest rubbish chute I've ever experienced. Then we – um –'

'You stole a car,' said Charlie, who knew because Sergei had told him.

'Well, er,' said Aneba.

'You stole a car,' repeated Charlie.

'Yes, well, we stole a car . . .'

'Ha ha!' laughed Charlie. 'You stole a car!'

'Yes, well, we went to Paris –'

'In your stolen car,' interrupted Charlie.

'Shut up, Charlie,' said Magdalen.

'You stole it too!' Charlie retorted.

'Enough,' said Aneba firmly, and, tempted though he was to carry on, Charlie recognized from his father's tone of voice that trouble was just one more cheeky answer away, so he let it drop. Reluctantly.

'We found the circus boat,' Aneba continued, 'and your friends Julius and Pirouette and Madame Barbue, and Mabel.' He didn't mention how much she and Magdalen had fought to start with, or how Mabel had been loyal to Maccomo. 'Mabel worked out that you'd be bringing the Lions here, and we followed. But – where *is* Maccomo? We expected him to be here too.'

Charlie hesitated.

Maccomo was tied up under a tree out in the Argan Forests, where the Lions lived. He was the Lions' prisoner. Charlie felt in his heart that Maccomo's fate was fair and not unreasonable, but he wasn't sure the grown-ups would agree. He'd worked out the fate with the Lions, who were

extremely tough and straightforward when it came to things like revenge and punishment. They didn't have any human delicacy. Perhaps his parents would want to take Maccomo to the police station or something respectable like that. In the old days the police, apparently, were who you relied on to sort out crime problems, and his mother could be very old-fashioned at times . . . but nowadays everybody powerful had a police force of their own. Security, they called them.

Also, he wondered how Mabel felt about Maccomo now.

But he had to tell them.

'He's with the Lions,' he said at last. 'It seemed only fair.'

Mabel gasped. Charlie knew what she was thinking: how would the Lions, his former prisoners, treat him now that they were in charge, in their own territory?

He gave her a straight look – as if to say, 'So? Your tigers, who you love so much – would they harm *you*, if you lost your power over them? And if they would, what does that tell you?'

Magdalen and Aneba glanced at each other.

Then: 'Good riddance,' said Aneba. 'We've got better things to worry about.'

Magdalen didn't look quite so convinced, but she let it pass. It didn't matter anyway. Charlie knew that no humans would take the Lions on, unless they were prepared to fight to the death – or unless they had Charlie to negotiate for them.

Mabel was quiet.

'Speaking of which,' said Magdalen, 'do we need to worry about Rafi? Where's *he* gone?'

'Exactly,' said Aneba. 'A bad arm and a punch in the face aren't going to get rid of him forever.'

'Well, anyway, we shouldn't stay here,' said Magdalen. 'Rafi knows we're here. He can tell the Corporacy. He might have told them already. We should go home and report all this and get some government protection and get back to work – there's still a lot to be done on the asthma cure –'

'Oh,' said Charlie. He reached into his pocket. 'Here.'

The piece of paper he handed his mum was battered and travel-stained. His feeling of pride at giving her back her asthma cure formula was pure and strong and joyful.

She blinked at it. 'Bless you,' she said, and gave him a blinding smile, followed by another blinding, passionate hug. 'We just need to get back to normal . . .' she said, and she drifted into silence.

Aneba was giving her a long, sad look.

'What?' she said.

Charlie understood. 'He means there isn't any normal any more,' he said.

Magdalen thought about their little house in London, their yard with its honey-scented plants, their neighbours. How safe and long ago it seemed. 'Oh,' she said.

'If we go home to London,' said Aneba gently, 'the whole

thing can just start up again. How could we live and be safe? I really think we should go down to Ghana, and take some time, and from there we can get in touch with people in London and see what's going on without returning to our usual haunts.'

For a moment Charlie imagined them all as ghosts, haunting their house and the market and the fountain where the schoolkids played football. He didn't want to be a ghost. He'd kind of thought it would all be over once he found his parents. They would take charge again, they'd all go home, and everything would – yes, he too had thought everything would go back to normal.

But now there was no normal. He could see that. There could be no normal until Rafi was definitely stopped and got rid of . . . But how can you definitely stop and get rid of someone? Kill them? He didn't want to kill anyone. And, more importantly, there could be no normal until the Corporacy was stopped and . . . But you can't get rid of something as big as the Corporacy. The Corporacy had business all over the world, it made and sold medicine all over the world, it had its weird Gated Village Communities all over the place, full of people living Corporacy Lives. People loved the Corporacy – it made the people inside feel safe. It was so big and powerful. Yeah, thought Charlie, it's so big and powerful, it thinks it can just steal people and make them work for it.

How were his parents ever going to get away from that?

It made his head spin.

'I think you're right,' said Magdalen. 'We'll go south. How about you, Mabel?'

'I'd really like to be with you all,' she said, 'and have a rest, which is what you certainly need. A lovely holiday . . . but I know that's not really on. No. I must go back to the Circus. I can't leave my tigers with Major Tib and Sophie forever.'

Charlie felt a pang of disappointment – here he'd just acquired this rather mysterious and glamorous aunt, and now she was disappearing again before he could even get to know her. And he wasn't sure he trusted her, even if his parents did. He felt bad as well about Major Tib, the tall, magnificent Ringmaster with his high boots and velvet tail-coats. He knew Major Tib was furious about the Lions escaping, but he liked him and respected him, and he meant him no harm.

'Tell him . . .' he said.

'Tell him what?' said Mabel in an amused tone.

'Tell him – tell him I was *for* the Lions, not *against* him,' said Charlie. 'Tell him I'm kind of sorry. And send my love to Julius and Hans and Pirouette and Madame Barbue and Sigi and everybody.'

Mabel smiled. 'OK,' she said. She recognized something in Charlie then. She had known already that he loved the Lions – that was obvious, by what he'd been through with them – but now she knew that he loved the Circus too. He was a good kid. Family. Her smile was a little wobbly.

Charlie stared at her. She still made him nervous.

She was glancing across at Magdalen.

'Magdalen,' she said. Then she took a big breath and sighed. And, abruptly, she said, 'Oh, snike it, so what – listen, all of you. This is it. What happened. Mag –' She breathed in a huge breath. 'Mag, I had a baby.'

She'd gone white, like an egg. Then she went pink.

Magdalen stared at her.

'I was pregnant and I took off and Mum didn't know and I had it adopted.'

Silence.

'It?' said Magdalen very quietly.

'Please don't judge me,' said Mabel. 'Him. I had him adopted. It seemed the right thing to do. Then everything was different for me and I couldn't go home and I never went home and I'm glad to be with you now. Please don't judge me.' The words tumbled out, a waterfall of words over sharp, difficult stones. 'I don't need to talk about it, or want to, but you need to know. I'm very, very sorry for deserting you.'

Charlie was confused.

'Surely if you're having a baby that's just when you need to stay home?' he said.

The women looked at him.

'Yeah,' said Mabel. 'I know that now. It looked different then.'

'Need to think about this,' said Magdalen. She looked a little ill.

Not having any brother or sister, Charlie didn't know much about that kind of family life, but he could easily see that if you had a sister and she'd just disappeared, you'd be a bit upset.

'Nothing to think about,' said Aneba, sitting up. 'It was long ago and you're both here now. Take some time to get used to each other again – Mabel, don't go yet. You and your sister need to hang out together.'

The two women were holding hands. Charlie caught Aneba's eye and Aneba winked at him and stood up, saying, 'So, Charlie, we're going to Ghana. See Grandma. Swim at Labadi Beach and Mile Thirteen. Go and watch the Starlets . . .' The Starlets were Charlie's favourite football team, the national juniors, and they'd been doing incredibly well recently, beating all the top junior teams.

Would Rafi and the Corporacy follow them to Ghana?

Still, at least Maccomo was dealt with.

CHAPTER TWO

Essaouira lies between the thunderous Atlantic, which pounds its dark red ramparts and purple rocks with huge waves, day and night, and a long, low, scraggly forest of argan and thuja trees, which grow out of the sand and smell delicious when you rub their tough spiny leaves. The forests used to cover most of the area, but the thuja wood when polished made pretty boxes and picture frames which smelt as bittersweet as the leaves, so every year there was less and less forest, and more and more pretty souvenirs for visitors. Luckily, a hundred years or so before, some carpenters had noticed that at this rate their grandsons would have no wood to make boxes from, and started replanting the forests. There was enough forest now for some parts of it to be forgotten and wild again, rough and thorny, inhabited only by snakes and lizards and owls and runaway goats – and Wild Lions.

It was from here that Charlie's Lion friends had been kidnapped and was to here that they had returned. (Only Primo, the ancient creature who had been created, not born, stayed behind in Venice, loved and adored by the Venetians.) The Oldest Lion had found that his mother was still alive, the three Lionesses had greeted their sisters, and the Young Lion and Elsina, who had both been born in captivity, shyly began to make friends with the wild cousins that they had never met. At night, they all lay together. Elsina's eyes were as round as the moon as she lay wakeful under the African night. She had never slept out of doors before leaving the Circus. She had hardly even *been* out of doors. The adventure – running through Paris with Charlie, hiding on the train roof through the dreadful snowstorm, their time locked up in the courtyard in Venice, the long trip on the solarboat – all that had been exciting and terrifying. But this was something different. This was meant to be home. This was, apparently, where she belonged.

She gazed up at the moon. The moon gazed down at her. She snuggled closer to her brother. He at least was unchanged.

The Young Lion snuggled back. He too was having trouble sleeping. Every night he kept one eye and a tiny portion of his mind always turned to the big tree to the east, where the Liontrainer Maccomo, their former master, was tied up. For years Maccomo had kept the Lions prisoner on board the *Circe*, drugging them with those scented drops he put in their water, forcing them to do tricks in the Ring, keeping them in that cabin . . . Now it was his turn. He was their prisoner, and they were drugging *him*.

The Young Lion had wondered how a bunch of Lions could give drugs to a human, but it wasn't hard. In the first place, Maccomo had developed a taste for the drops after Charlie had started giving him the medicine to make him dopey, way back on the *Circe*. So when the Oldest Lion stood in front of Maccomo with the bottle between his feet, and his paw lazily lifted, studying his long, terrible claws, revealing them and then sheathing them, and giving Maccomo a look, it didn't take long for Maccomo to get the idea. The Lions wanted him to drink the drops. Fair enough. He was so tired and shocked and terrified that he couldn't even think about what a dreadful situation he was in. Taking drugs to blur his mind seemed to him like a very good idea. Well – to part of him. The part of him that was blurred already . . .

'Poor, stupid Maccomo,' said the Oldest Lion, looking at him with contempt.

'Father,' said the Young Lion. 'Two things worry me. He might drink it all and kill himself . . .'

'That worries you?' said the Oldest Lion. 'How would that be a problem?'

Looked at Lionishly, of course, it was not a problem.

'You've been too long with Charlie,' said the Oldest Lion. 'That's a human thought, a human fear. Lions don't care about other things dying.'

He's right, thought the Young Lion. I'll have to think about that.

'Your other point?' the Oldest Lion was saying.

'What do we do when it runs out? Won't he become strong again, and try to escape?'

'He will never be healthy, living here, eating the bits of flesh we give him. This life in the Lions' place will make him weak, just as life in the human place made us weak. We need not fear him.'

But the Young Lion was not sure. Even tied to a tree, suffering with the heat of the sun in the day and the cold of the forest nights, even weak, and drug-addled, and badly fed, Maccomo was still Maccomo. He was still a clever, calm, mysterious man, a man with a bad, selfish, cunning heart. He was not to be underestimated.

Far away in Venice, Primo was sad. He felt safe, living with the pale statues and the tall lamps in the great courtyard of the Doge's Palace – well, what *had* been the Doge's Palace but was now, since the Doge's removal from power, the Palace of the People of Venice. He ate well; he was warm. Venetian cats came each day to talk to him. Venetian humans came too, asking for his blessing on this and that, and he gave it, and that seemed to make them happy. The noble gondoliers tended to his every need: Claudio, of course, and Gabriele, Alessandro and Carlotta.

But he was sad. He missed the only companions he had ever known, the group of Lions who had taken him in and helped him, with their curious human boy, Charlie. He was old, he knew it, and he was tired. He didn't really like being looked at. No amount of cushions and admiration could make Venice's damp rotting islands hot and dry. Lapping waves were not rustling grasses. These humans were not the lizards and goats of . . . of where?

Primo was homesick for a home he had never known. He had made his decision to stay in Venice for the best of reasons – if in the height of excitement – but actually, in his ancient heart, he wished he were . . . where? Well. The only home of the only Lions he had met was Africa. He wished he were in Africa, with them.

Claudio noticed. He saw that Primo wasn't really eating properly, that he no longer swayed to his feet when visitors came to see him, that he tired quickly. Claudio did his best by bringing Primo fresh red meat, by letting him sleep, by singing to him and playing the piano – Primo loved music – but it was no good. When Primo, after refusing food for three days, developed a cold and started sneezing, Claudio could avoid the truth no longer. They should have gone with the others.

Claudio's Song for Primo

R. LOCKHART

One morning, assuming his special Talking-to-Lions position (standing rather formally with his head slightly bent and his hands clasped in front of him) and speaking very clearly, because he still did not quite believe that cats could understand humans, Claudio announced, 'Today,

Signor Primo, beloved of Venice, visitors is coming for you, to give you compliments and so forth.'

Primo wasn't that interested in visitors. He gave a heavy, breathy, Lionish sigh, and then he yawned, his immense sabre teeth arching from his mouth as his lower jaw dropped away. Claudio's eyes widened with admiration.

'Is no ordinary visitors,' continued Claudio. 'Is the man you didn't like because he keep you prisoner but now we know is only because he didn't understand properly his duties and now he very sorry – is, in fact, Edward, head of security services of King Boris of Bulgaria.'

Edward, eh? Edward, who had first dressed him up in the fake wings that the Venetians had so adored. Edward, who had kept Charlie and the Lions locked up in King Boris's palazzo for weeks when King Boris had said they were guests who needed help on their way to Africa . . . Primo turned his head away with a sniff.

But the man who approached him next was not Edward. Edward was a tall, fair Englishman with a very suave manner. This was a dark, bustling little man in a waistcoat the colour and sheen of a particularly glamorous beetle.

'Lead me on, lead me on!' he was crying as he crossed the courtyard. 'Where is the darling creature? Has he taken over the old devil's private apartments? Is he lying in glory on some damask-draped four-poster bed? I do hope so. If I find after all that he's living on damp straw in a back alley I shall be most disappointed . . .'

'Indeed, Your Majesty, he is not,' said the tall, fair Englishman who accompanied him. 'I am assured he is most carefully attended to, and —'

'I'm joking, Edward,' said the man. 'Can't you tell?'

'Of course, Your Majesty,' said Edward sheepishly, but at that moment Claudio approached and said, 'Your Majesty! I didn't know you was coming to Venice! Welcome, *benvenuto*, Majesty! Look, here is Primo. Primo, here is His Majesty.'

And Primo turned his head back.

Now, Primo and King Boris had never actually met. When Charlie had introduced the King to the Lions on board the Orient Express, Primo had stayed behind. Primo had been too huge, too strange, too sick, too sad to just go about meeting people. But now was different. Primo knew who King Boris was — his saviour, and the saviour of the other Lions and Charlie. And King Boris knew who Primo was — the miraculous creature, created illegally from fossilized DNA, out of time and without family, the friend of the Lions and the Catspeaking boy, and the new mascot of Venice. But seeing him in life — how huge he was, his great teeth resting against his black gums, his massive shoulders and golden flanks — King Boris was swept over by a flood of admiration. What a wonderful animal.

'*Salve*, Primo,' said the King. 'How are you?'

Of course, King Boris could not speak Cat. But he knew Charlie could, and he was open-minded about these things, and a naturally friendly person.

Primo slowly blinked his huge eyes. They were milky and old-looking.

'Claudio,' said King Boris in a serious voice. (He had known Claudio since he was a small boy – indeed Claudio's dad had been King Boris's dad's personal gondolier. Claudio and he used to go scrumping pomegranates and fishing together as lads.) 'Claudio, he does not look well. Look how sad his eyes are. Look how he lies there, so tired and limp. What is the matter with him?'

'Your Majesty,' said Claudio, 'I wish I knew. It seem to me he is . . .'

'Is he eating?' asked King Boris. 'Sleeping well? Pooing and all that? Here – let me see his tongue.'

Primo, rather surprised, stuck out his tongue. It was pale and furry-looking.

'It should be pink and gleaming!' exclaimed King Boris. 'Have you had a vet in?'

'Yes, Your Majesty,' Claudio said. 'And he didn't know what was wrong. Such a strange creature – and you know I couldn't tell him the history of the creature, you know, in case bad people come and try to take him away – let them try! – anyway . . . Your Majesty, I think I know what is wrong.'

King Boris gazed thoughtfully at Primo, who had lain down again and closed his eyes. His nose was a bit dry.

'I think I know too,' said the King. 'What do you think, Claudio?'

'Sad and lonely and homesick,' said Claudio.

'Exactly,' said King Boris. 'So we must take him home.'

Claudio broke into a great smile. Of course!

'How?' he asked.

'Well,' King Boris continued, 'I was anyway going to say to you . . . Perhaps Edward would explain . . .'

Edward had been much chastened by his mistakes in dealing with Charlie and the Lions. He was actually very, very sorry that he had got carried away in the wrong direction, trying to use Charlie and the Lions to chum up with the Doge, instead of sending them on to Africa like he should have. King Boris had wondered long and hard about trusting him again after that, but one fact remained: Edward was better than anybody at getting information. And King Boris loved information. Knowing things was vital to him. So he had decided to trust Edward again – a bit.

'Of course, Your Majesty,' Edward began, rather pompously. 'Information has reached me of developments in the search for the kidnapped scientists Aneba and Magdalen Ashanti. They escaped, you recall, from the individuals who had – ahem – overenthusiastically requested their services, and made their way to a location whereat they considered their son, Charlie, would be likely to join them, and indeed that reunion has, we are informed, taken place.'

Claudio, listening very carefully, managed to work out what this meant: Charlie had found his parents.

'*Fantastico!*' he shouted, jumping up and punching the air.

Primo quietly smiled behind his whiskers. Good.

'However,' Edward murmured, and Claudio stopped jumping up and down. 'The reunion is under threat. The boy Sadler, Rafi Sadler, has removed himself from the hospital in Paris and taken himself to the same spot. It is believed that the missing Liontrainer, Maccomo, is also in the neighbourhood. The safety of the scientists and the boy –'

King Boris interrupted. 'Claudio, this idiotic family is just staying in a hotel there as if they were on holiday and they seem to have no idea how much danger they are in. The Corporacy wants them back – they don't care how. Sadler and this Maccomo are both, as far as we know, at liberty, and likely to seek revenge or recapture – or both. But never mind them – the Corporacy has far more efficient and powerful methods of getting what they want, and are likely to bring those methods into play now. Charlie is in danger – grave danger. I was going to send you down there to find out their plans, bring them back, guard them, talk sense into them – whatever it takes.'

'So . . .' said Claudio.

'You should take Primo,' said King Boris. 'The other Lions live just nearby. Drop him off, and then sort Charlie out.'

Claudio gulped.

'Take the balloon,' said King Boris. 'Much quicker.'

The Chief Executive of the Corporacy Gated Village Community at Vence was not a happy man. The two scientists, Ashanti and Start, had disappeared without a trace.

Rafi Sadler, who was meant to have got hold of their
child, to ensure their cooperation, was not returning his
calls. The whole Gated Community was upset – people
were asking why they would want to leave! Questions like
that – well, any questions really – were not a good sign.
Everybody had to be happy! To embrace their aspirations –
but that did *not* include aspirations to leave the Corporacy.

And, worst of all, news of the disruption had reached
Corporacy Headquarters. The Head Chief Executive had
been on the phone to him. He wasn't happy at all. Incidents
like this were bad for business, bad for morale, bad for
profits, bad for the Corporacy. These people were meant
to be living happily as part of the Corporacy Community,
not rushing about the place doing what they wanted! They
must be brought back and made to be happy!

Well. The Chief Executive had given Rafi Sadler his
chance. Rafi had brought the parents in, it was true, with
his 'I know the family, they'll believe me,' and his extremely
talented sniffer dog. But he'd blown it.

The Chief Executive picked up his telephone. Now it
was time to bring in the big boys. Corporacy Intelligence
and Security would deal with this themselves. They had to
get all three of those troublemakers in as soon as possible.
And the boy Sadler as well, just to be sure.

At the top end of Essaouira is a malodorous area, where
the poor people live – too poor to have anyone take the

rubbish away, too poor to keep their houses upright. Rubble litters the street where houses have collapsed. Damp from the sea seeps up rickety walls, bringing sickness to the children who live inside. Rats scurry about, and six or eight people sleep in any room with a roof still complete.

Rafi Sadler, running from his fight with Charlie, ducking and dodging to get away before Aneba came out, had swiftly become lost in the tangle of streets in the Medina, the walled old town. Before long he had found himself among the rats and the rubbish and hollow-eyed children.

His arm, weak anyway from where the Lioness had savaged him in Paris, and only partly healed, flamed with new pain as he ran. His jaw ached where Charlie had whapped him. But worst of all was his heart. Shame – hot, flooding shame – brimmed out of it and engulfed him. Charlie had beaten him! Him, Rafi Sadler!

He had tripped over something, and fallen to the ground. His shoulder jarred again. The pain was monstrous. Panting, heart pounding, he lay there. Something smelt horrible.

He realized that he was crying.

He let himself. Never had he felt so low.

To the young woman who had found him lying there, he didn't look so low. He didn't look as if he were suffering especially – she had seen too much suffering to be impressed by this. No, he just looked European – which meant that he would have money. True, he did look down on his luck, for a European. So she would help him, and then he would pay her. No problem.

'Come, I'll look after you,' she'd said to him, speaking in a mixture of French and Arabic. 'My name is Leila. Come.'

And so Rafi had been hauled painfully to his feet and taken into a dark, damp house to be helped.

Under the wide spreading tree at Lionhome, Maccomo was pretending to be asleep. He did this most of the time. His head lolled back in the dust and he let flies settle at the corner of his mouth. He wanted the Lions to think he was drugged and incapable. They did think it. When they passed, they looked at him in disgust. He watched them, motionless, from under almost-closed lids. Even his eyes seemed dusty and hot and half dead.

Only the Young Lion didn't trust him. The Young Lion, perhaps because he had been born in captivity, perhaps because of his closeness to Charlie, was more sensitive to movements of the human psyche. The Oldest Lion and the Lionesses were happily reverting to their wildness, remembering from before how it was to be a Lion in the forest. For them it was easy, and welcome, and wonderful. For the Young Lion, and Elsina, it was different. They had no previous experience of wildness to fall back on, no memories of how to be. They had to learn to hunt. They had to learn who the other creatures were with whom they shared the land. They had to learn how to tell good water from bad, good prey from bad, how to tell where you were. They had lost touch with the instincts that told them what the smell of the wind meant, or the shape of a footprint in the sand.

But they did know about humans, and they did not forget.

This is why it was a great shame that the Young Lion and Elsina were both away on a hunting trip the night that Maccomo made his escape.

He was not taking the drug. It had not been easy – part of him cried out for the ease of semi-consciousness, for the retreat from knowledge and pain, for the sheer soft comfort of not being . . . But he knew where he was, and he knew why, and he could not bear it. So each time the bottle was rolled towards him by a Lion paw, and he took it and put it to his mouth, he resisted. With enormous effort, he closed his parched lips against the drug, and only pretended to swallow the drops that would knock him out. Each time, he wanted to give up on reality, and accept that he would die a drooling idiot tied to a tree. But each time, the thought of Charlie made him strong. That boy would not beat him. That boy would not make a fool of him and destroy his life. He was Maccomo, the greatest Liontrainer, a man of power and mystery and reputation. This was not how he would die.

So at night when the moon was low and the Lions were sleeping, and sometimes even in the heat of the day while they took their siesta, he pulled himself towards a nasty, angular stone beyond the tree and, holding it in place between his feet, he rubbed the rope that bound his hands against its sharpest edge. The rope was thick, and the stone small, but Maccomo was determined, and the nights were long. If a Lion came near, he would let himself droop over the stone like a drug-sodden fool. He wasn't scared. Lions don't understand about tools. Only humans understand about tools. That's why they were able to have power over animals in the first place. They have no claws, no tusks, no poison, no swift legs to chase with or sharp teeth to bite with; they're not big like an elephant, strong like a hippo, or armoured like a crocodile; they can't crush like a boa or spit venom like a cobra, or fly away like a bird, or snarl like a wolf – they're just little soft naked creatures, with a brain to invent tools and hands to make and use them. And with those things they took over the world.

So, using his brain and his hands, Maccomo gradually wore through the rope that bound him. Then one night when there was no moon, and the Lions slept, he rubbed smelly Liondroppings all over him to disguise his human scent, and he set off west through the forest, following the last glow of the sunset and keeping the High Atlas Mountains behind him.

If the Young Lion had been there he would have had half an eye on Maccomo and it would never have happened. But he wasn't, and it did.

CHAPTER
THREE

A neba went on the Internet to plan their journey across the Sahara to Ghana. Solartrain to Marrakesh, then they'd have to cross the High Atlas over to Ouarzazate and Zagora, pass into Algeria – they'd be on camels by then. There was a Tuareg in Beni-Abbès who knew where the landmines were and could guide you through the rebel country . . . Fifty-two days to Timbuktu . . . Cross the River Niger, avoiding the feverswamps . . . Or maybe take the Route du Tanezrouft, through Mali – fewer people took it, so it would be safer – 1,300 kilometres of sand . . . Then was there a train from Gao? Otherwise Ouagadougou . . . He was busy with maps and timetables, secretive because he didn't want word getting out of where and when they were going. 'We don't know where young Rafi is,' he said. 'We must be careful.'

This carefulness, it had to be said, was driving Charlie mad. It wasn't that he didn't understand the need for it – of course he did. Hadn't he rescued a pride of Lions from the giant circus ship? Hadn't he plotted with gondoliers and an extinct sabre-toothed Lion to bring down the Doge of Venice? Hadn't he been imprisoned by the head of the Bulgarian Secret Services, and been snowed in on the Orient Express? Hadn't he seen off both Rafi Sadler, the teenage kidnapper, and Maccomo, the mysterious Liontrainer? Of course he understood about danger. Why couldn't his parents understand that, and stop — well, actually this was what really got him — telling him it was his bedtime?

Oh, it wasn't just that. It was the whole thing: stay in the hotel, Charlie; don't talk to Sergei outside, Charlie (which was a bit much, given that Sergei wasn't allowed in); no, you can't go to the beach, Charlie. But most of all: Charlie, it's your bedtime. He was practically taller than his mother, for crike sake. Weren't there rules about how they couldn't send you to bed after you were a certain height?

And another thing: they kept saying they didn't know where Rafi was. He could tell them. If they let him out for five minutes he could find Omar, the leader of the Essaouira cats, and Omar would track him down in no time. Or he could ask Sergei to ask Omar.

'No,' said his mother. 'I know it's hard, love, but we mustn't risk it.'

So he was imprisoned again! Every time he had anything to do with grown-ups they just imprisoned him. Even his parents.

He got pretty upset about it.

'But Rafi knows we're staying here!' he said. 'If he was going to tell the Corporacy he would have rung them days ago. They could be on their way here right now!'

'All the more reason to get away quickly,' said Aneba.

'Shouldn't we at least go and stay somewhere else?'

'Best to keep our heads down,' said Magdalen.

Charlie just didn't agree. He was pretty sure Rafi had left town – otherwise wouldn't Sergei have come and told him? Sergei would be talking to Omar, surely.

Charlie had searched the hotel for an outward-facing window, but everything faced in towards the courtyard. Except for the front, the walls were all party walls with other buildings.

There must be somewhere, he thought. On one occasion he tried to climb out on to the roof via the top balcony round the courtyard, but the hotel manager spotted him and called him down.

The one good thing about being stuck in was that he got the chance to talk to his new aunt. Of course, they talked about big cats. She was full of questions and Charlie was happy to have an opportunity to discuss Lions openly, and with someone who knew a bit about the subject. He held forth at such length that, though Mabel was delighted to listen, he felt it time he asked a question of her. He asked about her baby. He wasn't that interested, to tell the truth, but he couldn't think of anything else.

'He'd be eighteen now,' she said.

'Eighteen!' exclaimed Charlie. 'That's not a baby!'

'No, darling,' said Mabel. 'People grow, you know.'

'So do you know where he is?' he asked, to cover his embarrassment. Of course he knew people grew.

'Still with the woman who took him,' she said. 'Martha Sortch. I never met her. I never saw him again. The adoption people insisted.'

For a moment Charlie didn't even notice. He was trying to imagine how his aunt might feel about that, and to be nice to her.

'Does it make you sad?' he asked.

'Yes,' she said. 'There's always this little gap.'

Then it hit him.

'Sortch?' he exclaimed.

'What?'

'Her name was Sortch? Martha Sortch?'

'Yes,' said Mabel. 'Why?'

Maybe there were two. It wasn't a common name, but . . .

'Where did she live?'

'In London,' said Mabel. 'Mag and I lived in the country then, so I went up to town and the hospital organized it. Why?'

'Nothing,' said Charlie.

But it wasn't nothing.

Martha Sortch was Rafi's mother's name.

*

Rafi, thanks to the young woman's tending, was much better – physically. Mentally, he felt dreadful. He was very glad the mobile phones didn't seem to work around here, so he didn't have to receive angry, humiliating phone calls from anyone at the Corporacy saying, Where is our item? Have you still not found it? They blamed him for not having delivered Charlie, because if they had Charlie they could get Aneba and Magdalen back. And it was true, he had lost Charlie over and over again.

Well, he wasn't a fool. Charlie was much brighter and braver than Rafi had expected. And stronger. And he had those bliddy Lions on his side. So, Rafi had to be realistic. He needed help.

Not for the first time, Rafi wished Troy were still with him. Nothing like a big dog to make a guy feel big himself. But Troy had deserted him in Paris, so there was no use thinking about *him*.

(In fact, Troy was in a dog pound at the very southern-most tip of Spain, having been picked up on the quayside, where he had spent three days mooning tragically after the ferry that Rafi had taken across to Morocco. But Rafi, like many disloyal people, wouldn't recognize loyalty if it bit him on the bum. Which, of course, Troy was unlikely to do, being so loyal.)

Lying on the grubby blanket that passed for a bed in Leila's hovel, Rafi thought things through.

It was easy, really.

He hadn't the money or the contacts to hire anybody, plus they all talked bliddy Arabic and French, not proper English. He couldn't trust 'em. No, the person he needed was the person he'd worked with before. The person who had been prepared to sell Charlie to him. The person who had also been tricked by Charlie, and didn't forgive him. The person who wanted his Lions back, who was nearby – yes, Maccomo and Rafi would make a very good team.

He'd go and find him.

He didn't want to run into Charlie's dad, though. Crike, the size of the man. And Charlie threw quite a whack himself, so crike knows what the dad would be capable of.

Rafi's arm felt a lot better. The bruising on his brow was going down. He was pretty sure he'd caught some kind of lice in this dump, though. Bliddy itchy. Never mind.

So where would Maccomo be?

He pondered.

'Leila!' he called. She stuck her head through the empty doorway from the other room.

'Any animal dealers in this town?'

He assumed she didn't speak English, so he explained by speaking really loudly.

'Animal. Dealers,' he mouthed. 'Market. Animals.' He made an animal noise, just to be clear.

Leila, like most Africans, in fact had phrases of many languages, and she soon worked out what the crazy foreigner was on about. Later that day she led Rafi down some nasty alleys to the nasty little home of Majid the Lioncatcher – the very man from whom Maccomo had bought the Oldest Lion and the Lionesses in the first place, years before.

The Lioncatcher, a scraggly dark little man as crooked as a thuja tree and just as tough, sent a small boy for mint tea, and crouched down, gesturing Rafi to sit. Leila stood quietly at the back, taking in what was going on. If her foreigner was engaging in business, she might want a part of it.

'So,' said the Lioncatcher, after many formalities which made Rafi rather impatient – greetings, enquiries after health, waiting for the tea and so on. 'How can I help you? Do you need animals? Reptiles, birds, eggs – or my own speciality, Lions?'

'Not Lions,' said Rafi. 'I need . . . a Liontrainer.'

The Lioncatcher's eyes sparked. 'Anyone in particular?' he asked.

'You know which one,' Rafi said. 'The one that was here recently.'

The Lioncatcher grinned. 'Liontrainers are very expensive,' he said. 'But I will make you a good price . . .'

Rafi jumped up and in one movement took the skinny little man by the throat. 'I want him,' he said quietly, 'and he wants me. It would be foolish to stand between us.'

He let Majid down to the ground again. The man blinked at him.

'Do not make me your enemy,' Majid said calmly. 'You

have enough enemies already. Go to the ship in the harbour called *Old Yeller*. Speak there to Capitaine Drutzel. Go now and your Liontrainer will come to you.'

Moments after Rafi left, Maccomo appeared from Majid's other room. His wrists were still raw where the ropes had been cut away, but all traces of Liondroppings had been washed off him, and a decent dinner of lamb and oranges and couscous had strengthened him.

'How interesting,' he said. 'How very interesting.'

He looked up. Leila was still standing in the corner. 'Who are you?' he said. 'What do you want?'

'I brought business,' she said. 'I seek my share.'

Majid laughed, and handed her a coin. 'Go away,' he said, and she pulled her cloth over her head and left.

'So,' said Maccomo. His eyes were bright and his languor fell off him like a robe slipping from his shoulders. 'So, Majid, how soon can *Old Yeller* be ready? I shall go to Capitaine Drutzel later. You go back to the Riad el Amira. Sooner or later they have to come out. Go, and bring them to me: either three, or two, or one – it matters not. If I have only one the others will follow. Go!'

Majid smiled, and took down his sack and his long fork with two prongs, good for pinning something down by the neck; his small grey gun for shooting darts with; the darts themselves, long and nasty and containing drugs that, when they pierce the skin, send a creature to sleep; his ropes, his chains, his big whip.

He was officially a Lioncatcher, but he wasn't fussy. He'd catch anything if the money was right. And, though Maccomo might not have had money now, he'd always been a good customer. And even Majid had heard of the Corporacy.

There was no chance really of Primo leaving Venice quietly. Claudio handled it: he put the word out through the gondoliers and their mothers, and all the Venetians quite understood that their beloved winged Lion had to go home. They turned out in droves across to the Lido, to wave him off, and to see the great scarlet and pink hot-air balloon in which Claudio would take him away. A small band came too, to serenade the departure of the beloved Lion of San Marco.

The huge balloon lay on the long white beach, flexing and writhing like an animal as the hot air from its blowers filled it up. If Charlie had been there, he would have wanted to run inside the balloon, and feel the warm wind in the strange translucent cavern of silk.

'It's cold up there,' said King Boris, busily unloading from the back of his rickshaw several cashmere blankets for Primo to be swathed in. 'The wind is good. Shouldn't take you more than a day or two. Supplies are all on board – rather good supplies too – and the navigation system has just been serviced so you shouldn't have any trouble.'

King Boris's
Balloon

Suddenly, the balloon whipcracked, and whipcracked again, and then, in a great swooping movement as the hot air stiffened it, it leapt upright. The crowd gasped. The whole contraption – the quivering balloon and the compact and luxurious covered basket hanging beneath it, in which the voyagers would ride – was securely tethered to the ground. Even so, it looked as if it might fly off any time it chose. The basket looked tiny against the vastness of the balloon, let alone the sky above and the journey ahead of them.

'In you get,' commanded King Boris.

Claudio carefully led Primo up the special little stairs into the basket. King Boris stared southward, down towards the grey, flustered Adriatic Sea. He took a big breath of sea air.

Primo was inside now, nestled in his blankets. Claudio was standing on the edge of the hatch through which one entered the basket, awaiting instructions for take-off. The musicians were craning their necks as they played their special sad Bulgarian farewell tune in honour of King Boris's generosity to Primo.

King Boris had a look on his face.

'Actually,' he said, 'I think I'll come too.' And with a dashing grin he leapt up the stairs and into his favourite spot by the pilot's controls – it was quite a surprising feat for so stout a gentleman. Then he pulled some levers, pushed some buttons and steadied himself against a rail. 'Hold on!'

The Sad Bulgarian Farewell Tune

he called to Claudio above the roar of the blowers.

The ropes and the staircase fell away beneath them as the great glowing balloon rose slowly and beautifully into the air, lurching a little in the freedom of the wind before it righted itself. It was a magnificent sight. The music fell away too and the crowd gasped once more – especially Edward.

'But, Your Majesty!' he called.

King Boris was not listening, or he couldn't hear. 'Come on, Claudio!' he cried, his shiny black eyes beaming enthusiasm. 'Come, my fellow balloonatic! Let's go and help that foolish boy!'

When the Lions realized that Maccomo had escaped, all hell broke loose.

'Who was watching over him!' howled the Young Lion. 'How could this have happened! All the help that Charlie gave us, and he only ever asked us to do one thing for him, and now we have failed!' He was overwrought.

'Calm down,' said the Oldest Lion. 'The mothers have already given chase.'

And indeed they had. Without a word to anyone, the three Lionesses had set off through the forest, long and swift and silent, trying to catch Maccomo's scent, trying to track him. But they were confused: just as in Paris the Yellow Lioness had peed to disguise Charlie's scent and confuse Rafi's dog, Troy, so the Liondroppings with which Maccomo had smeared himself now confused them. When for a moment they thought they had caught his track, they were then filled with doubt by smelling – themselves. They ran hither and thither, following now one of their brothers, now one of each other, but never – quite – Maccomo.

The Wild Lions – those who had never been in captivity – looked on, a little puzzled at all the fuss. They understood that their ex-captive brothers and sisters felt a debt to the human Catspeaking boy, but it would have been a darn sight easier just to have eaten this Maccomo in the first place – it would have avoided all sorts of trouble. If he'd gone, good riddance to him. Someone would eat him soon enough anyway.

The Oldest Lion, though it took him longer to come round to it, somewhat shared this point of view. Maccomo could hardly survive in the forest. The mothers would catch him. Charlie would be long gone by now anyway. There was nothing they could do, if they failed to find him now. They would keep looking, of course.

'Keep looking for how long?' asked the Young Lion. 'And in the meantime – what if Charlie has not left? And even if he has – he believes that he is safe from Maccomo. He will go out into the world believing that we are protecting him by keeping Maccomo prisoner, and not only are we *not* protecting him, we haven't even told him that we're not. Let me go after him, Father – after Charlie – to tell him what has happened.'

'I'll go too,' said Elsina.

'Don't be stupid,' said her brother. 'Father, let me go.'

The Oldest Lion looked down at his son with great affection. 'No,' he said.

'But I must,' said the Young Lion. 'I must – I mean, I must. I have to.'

'No,' said the Oldest Lion.

'Why not?'

'You'll die. You'll be caught. You won't find him. You'll be alone and helpless. You'll be taken back to the Circus, or to a zoo, or killed for your fur, or so someone can eat your flesh.'

'You mean I am too young –'

'I mean you are too Lion – you are too animal. Only humans and birds can travel around without protection nowadays. I have not brought you out of captivity to lose you again.'

'Charlie brought us out of captivity, Father,' said the Young Lion quietly.

The Oldest Lion turned away. 'Do not think I am happy about this!' he snapped. 'You are not going. Anyway, the man is drugged and weak. The mothers will find him soon and bring him back.'

The Young Lion was not convinced. He had a reason of his own for knowing better: he had checked the medicine bottle, rolling dusty by the wide old tree. Dusty, forgotten, and not much emptier than it had been when they took it off Maccomo in the first place. Maccomo was not drugged and weak. He was strong, determined and full of plots. No way could he be left to go after Charlie, and Charlie not be warned.

A day or two later, the goats and lizards and Wild Lions of the Argan Forests were astounded by the sight, just before dawn, of an enormous scarlet globe with what looked like a giant nest slung beneath it sliding slowly across the pearly sky, roaring softly as it went.

'What on earth is that?' wondered Elsina, lifting her head from drinking at one of the forest's few streams.

'It looks like the *Bucintoro*,' said the Young Lion. 'Like the glories of Venice . . .'

For a moment he and Elsina silently remembered their curious past: King Boris's palazzo, the Doge's great scarlet and golden boat, the murky canals and elegant black gondolas of Venice.

'It's beautiful,' said Elsina.

'It's nothing special,' said one of the Wild Lions, irritated by talk of things he knew nothing about. 'It's just some big bird.'

The Young Lion and Elsina exchanged glances. This always happened when they mentioned human stuff. That's why they usually kept quiet about it. Silently they lowered their heads and turned back to their drinking.

And that is why they did not notice when, about five miles on, the balloon began to descend, nor when it landed, with a thud and a lurch like a huge octopus swaying on the tide. The bright silk collapsed sideways over a thicket of thorns, bouncing slightly. A long mottled snake shook and slithered swiftly away. Lizards skittered. Birds rose in clouds from the thuja trees, cackling and twittering in fear.

Within moments, one brave little goat had hopped up

on to a branch of thuja and was trying to nibble the silk. Seconds after that, King Boris appeared at the hatch, calling, 'Dear goat, desist! This is a mode of transport, not dinner! For goodness' sake, foolish beast, go and dine elsewhere!' The goat, too stupid to be alarmed, gave King Boris a friendly look and went back to nibbling.

Claudio appeared behind King Boris and peered out. Together they emerged and clambered to the not-very-high top of the tree.

'There is the town,' said Claudio, pointing off to the west, where Essaouira was beginning to show up, a smudge on the flat horizon in the early light. 'I shall go and find Charlie. He'll be able to take Primo safe to the Lions.'

'And I shall stay and guard the balloon,' said King Boris. It had started to flex and sway as if it were thinking of taking off again. 'From goats.'

'*Ciao!*' called Claudio. 'I be quick as I can!'

CHAPTER FOUR

That very morning, Aneba and Magdalen had to go to the Consulate to sign for papers permitting them all to cross into Algeria and Mali and Burkina Faso. No, they couldn't have the papers sent to the hotel. Yes, they both had to come. No, there was no other way. Sorry, madame. Sorry, monsieur.

Aneba, aware of how recognizable they looked together – the huge African and the red-haired woman – decided they should go separately, but at the same time, keeping an eye on each other. He wore a burnoose, a long Moroccan robe, its hood pulled up over his head. She wore a hat and sunglasses. Charlie was instructed to STAY PUT.

Moments after they left, he scurried out to look for his friends. Freedom at last! Where was Sergei? If he were around, Charlie wouldn't even have to go out. No sign of him.

He wanted to talk to Sergei about Rafi being his cousin. He hadn't told Magdalen and Aneba. Why not? Because he knew, in some deep and inexplicable way, that the news would really hurt them. He also knew they'd find out in the end. Perhaps it was cowardly of him, but he didn't want to be the one to tell them. Or Mabel. But he was desperate to confide in someone. So where was Sergei?

Charlie swiftly headed down towards the harbour. He was pretty sure that was where he would find Sergei or Omar – any cat, basically. He took the back alleys, wary of being seen. He had to come out by the café, though, and as he passed he looked for Ninu.

Of course he couldn't see him – Ninu was a chameleon, after all. But then a tiny voice called out, 'Hey, boy!'

Charlie ducked into the shadow of Ninu's creeper.

'Hi there,' he said. 'Have you seen Sergei?'

'Headed down to the harbour about ten minutes ago,' said Ninu. 'Why? What's up?'

Ninu liked to be involved in things. He liked to help, if he could. He liked to feel helpful.

'We're leaving,' said Charlie. 'Going down to Ghana – crossing the Sahara! My parents have gone to get the papers now; that's why I could get out.'

'Oh,' said Ninu. His eyes turned down. He looked sad.

Charlie stroked him under the chin. 'What's the matter, Ninu?' he asked.

'You're the only one who replies when I talk,' whispered the chameleon. 'I like you . . . and I want to tell you –'

'I'm sure we'll meet again,' Charlie said. 'I've got to go now. Got to find Sergei. I'll come back, though!'

Charlie gave Ninu a grin and ran on down towards the harbour.

He was just approaching the quiet, empty corner by the disused bathhouse, near the fishmarket dump, where no doubt Sergei would be, when he realized just how big a mistake he had made.

Out of the blue – out of the bright shining seaside day, full of sun and gulls and surf – a rough-textured smelly darkness descended on him. He was grabbed. He was bundled. Now he was lying squashed in a restricted space, with a sense of quick trundling beneath him.

It only took seconds.

He fought, he struggled, he yelled.

It made no difference. The rough cloth was almost in his mouth. It was tight and he couldn't move his hands to brush it away. It smelt horrible. Tasted horrible. Trundle, trundle, trundle, busily along an uneven road. It hurt, bang-bang-bang on his elbows and hips and head.

He hadn't even found Sergei.

He was all alone.

Oh, god. What were his parents going to say?

He'd been a fool. He knew it immediately – he'd been a fool.

Ninu liked the café. He enjoyed watching humans come and go, trying to guess by their hair and their clothes which human language they would speak – Arabic or French, Riffi or Tamazight or Tashelhait, or English or German, Japanese, Italian or Spanish, plus the African languages, of course, Bambara or Dioula, Fon or Hausa, Wolof, Hassaniya, Malinké, Tamashek, Crioulu . . . not that it made any difference. Any language that came by, human or animal, Ninu slipped into as easily as he slipped into a different colour when he sat in a different place.

But what was the point of knowing all the languages, and hearing all the conversations, when no one would talk to *him*? Most of the time, they didn't see him, they didn't hear him . . . Ninu was used to being ignored. Especially by adults.

He was sorry the boy who responded was going away. He had chatted a bit with that scruffy cat friend of his. He wanted to talk to him about the wicked Lioncatcher and the man with the hood who had waited for weeks for a boy, an unusual boy, to arrive on a ship . . . He had wanted to tell him about the conversations he had overheard between them. He wanted to know if it were true what the cats said, that the boy had brought back the captive Lions who had returned to the forest, and to tell him what a passing sparrow had just told him, about the gigantic red thing that had arrived in the forest that morning, which breathed fire and hot air like a dragon and had foreign humans aboard . . .

He sat in his plant (green for the leaves, turning a bit purple on one leg for the flowers) and watched. Who was this fellow now? Tall and blond, northern-looking, and speaking English, though with a very funny accent, chatting with the waiter.

He was asking about the boy.

Ninu cocked his scaly green ear.

'An English African boy,' he was saying. 'Brown, maybe have a cat with him . . .'

'The hungry boy!' said the caféguy. 'The boy who wanted to buy all my raw meat.'

Claudio smiled. 'That's him!' he cried. 'Where can I find him?'

'Don't know,' said the caféguy. 'Some days since I see him. Maybe he is gone.'

'Where did he stay, do you know?' asked the blond man.

'I don't know,' said the caféguy. 'Sorry.'

Actually, he did know. But he'd grown to like Charlie, and he didn't like Maccomo or the Lioncatcher, and he didn't know who this new guy was, and so he wasn't going to say anything any more to any of these guys who came asking about that boy.

He went back inside.

Ninu looked at Claudio. He wasn't a very brave creature, but he was curious. He knew the boy had been in Venice – Sergei had mentioned it. This guy sounded Italian to him. Slowly, Ninu approached down a long grey branch.

'Hello,' he said gently, in English. His accent was coming out like the man's.

'*Scusi?*' said the man, surprised.

A response! Ninu was delighted. A sensitive person! And definitely Italian.

Ninu spoke to him in Italian this time. 'You're asking about the boy,' he said. 'Who are you?'

The Italian stared at him. He looked a bit ill, suddenly.

Here we go, thought Ninu. 'Yes, I can talk,' he said. 'Amazing, isn't it?'

'Yes,' whispered Claudio. 'Amazing. But many things are amazing.'

Well, that's true, thought Ninu. Perhaps this man had some sense, even if he was an adult. He was about to proceed with the conversation, when suddenly a hurtling blur of fur leapt on to the terrace. It was Sergei, his hair all on end, screeching, 'Ninu! Oh, my fat aunt – Claudio! What the bliddy crike are you doin' 'ere?'

The Italian jumped up. 'Sergei!' he cried out, then: 'Oh – little reptile, can you speak Cat? Quick, what is he saying?'

'He's saying why is Claudio here and that we must go to the hotel,' said Ninu, alarmed and fascinated.

'Tell him –' said Claudio, but Sergei was still talking, quickly and urgently.

'Ninu – tell him that Charlie has been pushed into a trolley by the Lioncatcher and is being taken on board a ship down by the harbour. Tell him to go and stop them – fight them. You come with me to the hotel – you must tell his parents.'

'They're not there,' said Ninu. 'They went to get papers for their travel.'

'No, no, no!' cried Sergei.

Ninu swiftly translated for Claudio, who turned even paler and said, 'Who is the Lioncatcher?'

Even before it had been explained that he was a crony of Maccomo's, Claudio was on his feet, with Ninu on his arm, running down to the harbour.

'Which ship?' he shouted wildly, looking at the small fishing boats and the little tugs and the barge that took tourists round the old prison island where the falcons nest now. 'Which ship, Sergei?' People were looking at him strangely.

In the excitement, Ninu fell off his arm. Sergei was right there beside him, staring about, trying to identify which of the boats had their precious friend aboard.

Ninu was scared down on the ground. Cats are quick, and people expect them. Chameleons are just vulnerable. He scurried up on to Sergei's back.

'Down there!' yelled Claudio, and sure enough at the very end of the harbour an old barque, junk-rigged, had its sail up and was beginning to manoeuvre away from the dock.

They hurtled down.

Claudio swore.

Sergei leapt.

Ninu clung on.

Claudio swore again.

The ship moved off.

Now, Claudio could have grabbed a nearby boat and tried to follow, he could have called for the police and explained the situation, he could have done many things, but he was in a difficult situation. For a start, there was King Boris, plus there was Primo, and above all somebody had to tell the boy's parents what was going on.

Claudio strode back to the café. The caféguy looked up as he marched in.

'The boy has been stolen,' Claudio said, without preamble. 'Where was he staying? Where are his parents?'

The caféguy saw the desperation in Claudio's eyes, and trusted him. 'Riad el Amira,' he said. 'Right, left, right, right, cut behind the fountain, left and right again.'

Claudio was there in minutes. They weren't back yet.

He caught up with them in the queue at the Consulate.

'Signora? Signore?' he said, politely but urgently.

They looked at him, at each other and back at him.

'I am Claudio, friend of Charlie from Venice. Gondolier. At your service.'

Magdalen smiled. 'He's spoken of you!' she said. 'How wonderful that you're here. Come on back to the hotel – he'll be so pleased to see you . . .'

Something in Claudio's face made Aneba put his hand on her arm.

'He has been taken on a boat, Signori, heading out to sea now. The cat Sergei and the little chameleon are with him. It is Maccomo the Liontrainer, and the local Lioncatcher, I believe. The boat is called *Old Yeller*. I couldn't follow. But they just left. Only ten minutes ago.'

Magdalen turned whiter than ever. Aneba's face darkened with anger. 'We'll get a boat,' he said. 'Follow them.'

'We'll just get everything together,' said Magdalen. 'I'll get all our money from the cash machine. Get our clothes. Food. Fishing rod. You get a boat, Aneba – see you on the quay as soon as possible.'

'Can you sail?' asked Claudio. 'Can you navigate? Do you know where they are going? How far?'

'We must leave while they're still in sight, and not lose them,' said Aneba. 'We must leave immediately.'

Claudio was torn. He wanted to offer to go too – but there was King Boris and Primo!

'I am sailor,' he said. 'I can come if you can wait – but you can't wait . . .'

'Why can't you come now?' said Aneba.

'I have something to take to the Lions,' said Claudio desperately. 'I won't be long.' But how was he going to get Primo to the Lions without Charlie's help? It was all going horribly wrong.

The distress was dreadful.

'Bloody Lions,' said Aneba. 'Bloody, bloody, bloody.' He looked as if he wanted to bash his head against the wall.

CHAPTER FIVE

Charlie lay in the darkness, in the bag, scared. That was all. Shivery, sick feeling. Itchy skin. Just scared.

This is my fault, he thought. I shouldn't have gone out, they told me not to, and I did, and it happened. I am stupid, stupid, stupid and I deserve whatever happens to me now. Just because I was with Mum and Dad I thought everything was all right again. I forgot. I was stupid.

He wasn't being trundled any more. There had been a lot of urgent movement, and he'd felt himself hoisted and lifted. Now there was, what? Not stillness, but comparative calm. It felt not that he was being moved, but that he was in something bigger that was itself moving. What? Train? Wagon?

He couldn't tell.

His nose was itching and running. His eyes were dusty. Any minute now his breathing was going to start tightening, he could tell.

He wriggled around a bit and felt for his asthma puffer in his pocket. At least it was a new one. He didn't know how long he'd be . . . away.

He took a puff, held it, felt his lungs relax again, breathed out.

And that was it. There was nothing else. He lay there, uncomfortable, scared, stupid.

'I must go,' Claudio said. 'Leave a message, when you leave. I follow. I help. I promise you this. Your boy is important. I help.'

Even through her distress, Magdalen looked surprised and pleased by his declaration. 'Thanks,' she said. 'We'll leave word.' And she raced upstairs to pack up, before paying the bill. Aneba was going to clean out the cash machine.

'Though we'll hardly need cash at sea,' Magdalen observed.

'You need cash to get to sea,' said Claudio.

By the time she got down to the dock fifteen minutes later, Aneba was deep in discussion with a tall, lugubrious fisherman.

'He says they were going to America!' he cried as she ran up.

'America! What kind of boat was it?'

'Like that one, but bigger,' said the fisherman, gesturing to a medium-sized oldish-looking fishing vessel, solar-powered and with sails.

'How could that make it to America?' cried Magdalen.

'Thor Heyerdahl went in a raft,' said the fisherman's

companion, but Aneba and Magdalen were not interested in that now.

'Can you take us – follow them?' asked Magdalen urgently.

'Madame,' said the lugubrious fisherman, 'Capitaine Drutzel is a crazy man. I would not wish to follow.'

'We can pay,' she said.

'What use are riches if you are drowned?' said the fisherman.

Aneba gritted his teeth.

Magdalen began to cry.

'Please,' said Aneba.

'To follow them wherever they go?' said the fisherman.

'Yes, and not to lose sight of them now!' said Aneba. 'Look – there they are. Please. Please, catch this tide, take us. Please.'

The fisherman broke into a wide smile.

'The power of the parent who seeks the child is very strong,' he said. 'My boat also is strong. Together we will cross the sea or whatever God has in mind for us.' He peered towards the horizon. 'We have one hour before they disappear – we can buy much food, much water, and then we leave and all will be good if God wills it. Please to go and purchase many dates, which are the food of God. My name is Suleiman. Fear not.'

King Boris sat on top of the balloon, his telescope to his eye and his shotgun on his knee. He had no intention of shooting anyone or anything if he could possibly help it, but he was an experienced fellow, and assassins of any kind could crop up anywhere.

He looked out over the forest, but he was thinking about Primo. The journey had been hard for him. Personally King Boris thought Primo should get out and soak up some sunshine, but he was so tired, and perhaps, King Boris thought, a little scared. He wouldn't know in whose territory they had landed. He would feel vulnerable. Perhaps he should go down and try to give Primo some water, but he did not really want to get too close to him. But just then, a rustle came up through the long golden grasses outside, and a shadow skipped across the land.

Down in the basket Primo's nose twitched. Danger.

Up on top, King Boris flicked his head round, looking, scanning.

Nothing – nothing he could see, anyway.

Behind him, ten or fifteen metres away, the grasses parted.

A golden shape streamed towards the balloon. King Boris sensed it and, turning to look, reaching for the telescope, he slipped and he slid and he fell.

King Boris screamed as he bounced down the side of the balloon, grabbing uselessly for something to catch on to. He flung himself forward as he hit the ground, calling out to God to be merciful. His mouth tasted dust. He closed his eyes.

Hot breath on his neck.

A hot tongue on his cheek.

'Eat me quickly,' he begged. 'Bite me somewhere that matters. Make it quick.'

His whole self was clenched. Something rolled him over.

'Yes, bite out my belly,' he prayed. 'Now, do it now.'

Something was stroking him, tickling him almost. It made little mewing noises.

'No, no! Don't play with me! Please!' he cried.

If only he had spoken Cat he would have understood the mewing: 'Hey look, guys – it's King Boris! What's he doing here? King Boris! Are you OK?'

It had not taken long for news of the giant crashed scarlet bird to reach the Lions. Most of the Wild Lions had twitched their ears and gone back to sleep, but a couple of the younger ones, and the Oldest Lion, the Lionesses, Elsina and the Young Lion, had all decided to slope over and have a look at it – and, in the case of Elsina, give King Boris the fright of his life.

The Oldest Lion ignored her. He was lifting himself slowly up into the basket, following the scent to where Primo lay.

When he saw him, he blinked and smiled a low leonine smile.

'My old friend,' he said. 'My old friend. How have you come here? What is this?' He was deeply, deeply moved. 'Come, we will take you to our home. You are tired. Come, you will stay with us.'

The Wild Lions looked on in amazement as the huge ancient cat, with his sabre teeth, emerged. What were the returned Lions producing now?

The Lionesses, Elsina and the Young Lion swiftly moved to the basket.

'Primo!' they cried, except Elsina, who bounced around crying, 'Grandpa! Grandpa's come!' Full of pleasure at seeing him again, they touched noses and twitched their tails. The Lionesses tried to help Primo out of the basket. 'You are staying, aren't you?' they murmured in their furry golden voices.

'Oh yes,' he said. 'Oh yes.'

Elsina was now sitting on King Boris, on whom, in her enthusiasm, she had landed mid-bounce. He was still moaning. She started giggling.

'Open your eyes, silly!' she said. 'It's only me! Come on! We met on the train, don't you remember?'

She pushed him gently, and tickled him. He continued to moan. In the end she started to sing. Charlie had tried to teach them sea shanties on their way from Venice, and Elsina had more or less been able to hold a tune, in quite a caterwauling fashion. Now she remembered the tune that Claudio always used to sing: his gondolier song.

She started to sing it.

'She's lost her mind!' cried one of the Wild Lions.

'Oh dear,' said the Oldest Lion.

'Shut up, Elsina,' said the Young Lion.

But it worked. King Boris stopped yelling, opened his eyes, and found himself staring at the pink-nosed, golden-furred face of Elsina, the beautiful girl Lion.

'Good lord,' he said. 'You're Charlie's Lions!' He cried out in delight, and flung his arms round her neck.

The Wild Lions hissed and took a step back. 'How many human friends do you have? How much of this must we put up with?' they cried.

The Young Lion, meanwhile, was bending and touching the ground before Primo. 'I am glad you are here,' he said. 'What news?'

'Yes, indeed,' said the Oldest Lion. 'What news?'

The Wild Lions stepped back again. They did not approve.

They approved even less when King Boris's phone rang, and he started up an urgent conversation with Claudio.

Luckily, King Boris was one of those people who, when they are surprised, repeat what is being said to them.

'What?' cried King Boris. 'Charlie's been kidnapped?'

At this the Young Lion leapt to his feet.

'On a boat? His parents are going off after him?'

Beginning to snarl, the Young Lion pounded the ground beneath him.

'The Lioncatcher?' cried King Boris. 'A friend of Maccomo's?'

The Young Lion turned to his father.

'You see, Father?' he roared. 'You see what has happened?'

All his cubbishness fell away from him – he was a young
Lion in his prime; he was strong and fearsome and extremely
angry.

King Boris dropped the phone in terror. Staring at the
Young Lion, he tried to edge away.

'Calm yourself,' said the Oldest Lion sternly, but *his* face
too had gone hard.

'Why, Father? Why is this a moment for calm?' He
turned his intent stare to King Boris, willing him to say
more.

King Boris bent gently to pick up the phone, not taking
his eyes off the Young Lion. 'Yes – yes, I'm still here . . .
No, the Lions sound upset . . . Yes, of course, you must go
. . . No, the balloon is damaged, we can't take it . . . I shall
come immediately . . . but the parents have already left,
you say? Claudio, listen – I shall come with you. Yes. Wait
for me. I shall come now. How are the tides . . .? Well, we
can still catch it then if I am speedy . . . Yes, no time to
lose. OK, at the harbour. Fine. *Ci vediamo presto.*'

'We can be at the port within the hour,' said the Young
Lion. 'King Boris walking will take too long.'

'And what will you do there?' said the Oldest Lion. 'Boy,
I know you want to help our helper, but what can you do?
A Lion, at sea? What can you do?'

'Father,' said the Young Lion, and his voice was
dangerous. 'Maccomo escaped from here. We promised to
keep him. Now Charlie is –'

'And what can you do about it? All of that is true, but what can you do about it?'

'I will bite in half every human in Essaouira until they send a ship after them and bring Charlie home safe, and Maccomo in chains!'

'And how will you tell every human in Essaouira that this is what you are doing? How are they to know the cause and solution to your righteous anger? How long before they shoot you, none the wiser as to your grief and guilt? Be wise, my son!'

The Young Lion looked to his father and said, quietly, firmly, 'Goodbye, sir.' He went and stood by King Boris, who flinched, but was watching carefully what was going on, and did not move away.

The Oldest Lion could not answer. He knew the Young Lion was doing what he had to. His face sank in a little as he said, 'Goodbye, my son.'

But when Elsina quietly, cautiously moved closer to King Boris too, and looked up at her dad, the Oldest Lion cried out, 'Don't be ridiculous, child. Come over here.' And the Young Lion gave a look so withering and scornful that she bit her lip.

'Don't even think about it, little girl,' he said. 'A little kid like you would only hold me back.'

She raised her head quickly, hot with indignation. Hold him back! What, him, the Great Hero! She knew what she thought of that. She remembered how brave and clever her mother and her aunts had been in the trek from Paris. Little girl indeed. But she stepped away from the King, back towards her father.

King Boris turned to the Lions, shaken and confused but exhilarated too by what had happened. 'Goodbye,' he said – only to find the Young Lion lowering his head and gesturing impatiently.

For a moment he didn't believe it.

Then he couldn't bring himself to believe it.

But when the Young Lion was still loping impatiently at his heels after ten minutes' scrambling over the dusty terrain, nudging him gently as to which direction to take, and every now and then lowering his head and front legs again, King Boris took all his courage in his hands and climbed on board. Still clutching his shotgun and his telescope, holding on tight with his knees, the King of Bulgaria raced on Lionback to Charlie's rescue.

CHAPTER
SIX

ergei and Ninu had landed on the deck with a splat, and immediately hid under a coil of rope.

Ninu squeaked.

'Shut it,' said Sergei.

'No need to be rude,' said Ninu.

'Shut it,' said Sergei again, and put his paw on Ninu's head.

'Mmph,' said Ninu.

Sergei bent down and stared into Ninu's eyes from his own level.

'Ninu,' he hissed. 'Shut cakehole, or I'll be compelled to masticate yer.'

Ninu shut it.

They lay in uncomfortable silence for some minutes. People were rushing about on deck, busying themselves as the boat left the harbour and headed out to sea. How many people? Sergei tried to peer through a gap in the ropes, but all he could see were feet, and they all looked the same, so he couldn't tell. They seemed to be travelling towards the sun — so, given the time of day, that meant they were going west. Well, they would be. There only is west, really. He'd keep his eye on it and see if they turned north or south later.

When it was dark, he'd sneak below and find Charlie.

What was he going to do with this bliddy chameleon, though?

Charlie lay in his bag, sniffing. He'd worked out that it was dark outside as well as inside his bag, therefore he must be inside somewhere because not enough time had passed for night to have fallen. The surface beneath him was hard but not cold – wood, perhaps, rather than stone. The air around him was stale. He was now engaged in trying to identify smells.

Sniff, sniff.

Beyond the strong smell of dusty sacking, there was something familiar about it. Familiar but strange. Dust, wood – could he be in a shed? No, there was the movement. A wagon? No, there was no fresh air. A covered wagon, a coach? No, the movement was wrong . . .

An industrial kind of smell, with a salty, oily thing in it . . .

A boat.

Once he thought of it, it was obvious.

OK, I'm on a boat.

Maccomo was safely out of the way, in the Lions' care. So it had to be Rafi who had grabbed him.

His cousin.

There was almost something funny about it. Rafi, chasing him around, wishing him harm, and sharing his blood. All these years and he'd never had a brother or a sister or anything, and now he gets a cousin, and it's Rafi. What a pathetic joke.

And how had Rafi managed to get hold of a boat? How had one-armed Rafi managed to manhandle Charlie into it?

Charlie was so angry. With himself for being so stupid, with Rafi for having got him. He was so angry, his whole face felt tight.

It's another round of the fight, he told himself. It doesn't mean Rafi's won, it's just another round of the fight. He began to think rationally through his situation.

One, where am I being taken?

Two, who's on board?

Three, someone will be along at some stage to feed me – presumably – which will in itself give me information.

His mind slipped easily back into the habits of being in danger, being on the run. Oh, but they weren't habits he wanted to have! He wanted to be safe. Yeah, well, you're not, he told himself. Get on with it.

Four, what do I have with me?

Aha!

Along with his medicine, shoved in his back pocket, he had his telephone. They'd all – he and his parents – got their vouchers charged up at the Riad el Amira. (Aneba, of course, had had to get a new phone.)

So was there any reception on this boat?

He wriggled his phone out of his pocket and switched it on. The turquoise light glowed weirdly in the dusty dimness.

He smiled.

So who would he call first?

Mum.

For a moment, as the ringing started, he felt full of hope. For a moment. Then: 'Hello, this is Magdalen Start, please leave me a message after the beep, thank you.'

Maybe there was no reception where she was. Or . . . Oh, it was useless to speculate. Just leave a message.

'Mum,' he hissed. 'It's me. I'm in a boat, in a sack. I'm OK, no idea what's going on. Somebody grabbed me, it must have been Rafi. I'll call you later if I can. Love you. I'm –' He had been about to say I'm sorry, I'm sorry, I'm so, so sorry, Mum, for being so stupid . . . But he found that his throat was choking up and his eyes seemed to be full of tears. No worrying them by crying, no way. No way. 'Bye, Mum – ring me. I've got it on vibrate. Bye.' He clicked off quickly.

Someone might come and take the phone off him. Better get a move on.

Dad? Well, they'd be together . . .

An idea struck him. What if they'd been grabbed too?

What if they were on the boat?

Or – what if they'd been separated?

He quickly pressed his dad's number.

Same thing, leave a message.

He recalled leaving a message on his dad's phone weeks, months ago, on the back step at home, the night they disappeared.

And now *he* had disappeared.

He left the same kind of message he'd left for Mum. But this time he did say sorry. He knew what it was like when someone you loved was snatched away from you, and he was miserable that he had inflicted this on his parents.

'Misery is not useful,' he said toughly. 'Not. Useful. Don't. Waste. Time.'

So then he rang Rafi.

While King Boris raced back from the forest, Claudio returned to the harbour.

Magdalen and Aneba had left. He could see their boat, *Suleiman's Joy*, moving off about a mile or so away. A neighbouring fisherman told him that yes, the African and the red-haired woman were on board.

'What's going on?' enquired one of the boatmen, a very cheerful, muscular little man in a grubby djellaba. 'All these sudden departures and chases.'

'What was the first sudden departure?' Claudio asked.

'*Old Yeller*,' said the boatman, and spat over the harbour wall. 'Nasty thing anyway.'

'And that one?'

'*Suleiman's Joy*,' he said. 'Good boat. Good man. Don't know where he thinks he's going, though.' He looked a little wistful.

'Do you have a boat?' asked Claudio.

'Of course,' said the boatman. 'I am a boatman, of course I have a boat.'

'Which?'

'Why? You want me to follow and chase too? Please! I can follow, I can chase, yeah, James Bond, cops and robbers, police and thieves. Are we the good or the bad? Or the ugly?'

'Are you equipped?' asked Claudio. 'It might be a long trip.'

'Can you pay? Then I am equipped.'

And thus the third Essaouira boatman of the day got an unexpectedly large and complicated job at short notice. But only this one – his name was Younus and his boat was called *El Baraka* – the Blessing – got a Lion as a passenger.

Charlie could hear the phone ringing. Sometimes it seems you can tell by the way a phone rings whether anybody is going to answer it. There's the close, warm, immediate ring, which you know will be picked up in seconds, and then there's the hollow echoing hum down the lines, which will never be brought to a close by a friendly human voice. This ring seemed to Charlie very close – well, of course: Rafi would be on the boat. Charlie had disguised his number, though – Rafi would not know who was calling.

It seemed *very* close, actually.

Suddenly Charlie realized why.

He was hearing the ring through his other ear: not the one he was holding to the phone, but the other one.

Rafi's phone was in the same place as Charlie was.

And then Rafi answered it.

''Allo? Who's that?'

And Charlie heard Rafi's voice, across the – the whatever it was he was in. It sounded like he had been woken.

Crike, that was close. Thank god he had talked so quietly when he'd left the messages for his parents.

But what was Rafi doing in the same place he was? Surely he would be on deck, or in some swanky cabin. Or was he, Charlie, in a swanky cabin?

No, he knew the smell of under the waterline. He was in the hold, he was sure.

So why was Rafi asleep in the hold?

And then there was a noise, a bang, footsteps.

A voice. 'Give me this, please. No telephone here.'

And Rafi's voice saying, 'No, I bliddy won't. I came here in good faith. I came here to do business. I don't know what you're playing at, but your boss is not going to be happy at you treating me like this . . .'

Charlie held his breath. Rafi was a prisoner too!

But then who . . .?

And then there were more footsteps, and then there was another voice, a smooth, gentle voice with a cold line of iron running right through it. A voice that Charlie knew very well.

'Don't be silly, Rafi,' it said.

And Charlie's blood ran cold to match. It was Maccomo.

At just around that time, sixteen men in two armoured limousines – petrolcars – drew up by the main gate to Essaouira. They were large, and they were wearing burnooses. They stepped out of the long cars and looked around them. Everyone was staring at the cars. Essaouira had not seen a petrolcar in years. One little boy burst into tears. Several women made the sign against the evil eye. A stallguy spat.

The men walked into town, not hurrying, not hesitating, and broke into pairs. They talked on their mobile phones, looking left and right. One pair went directly to the Riad el Amira. One went to Maccomo's lodgings. One went to Ninu's café, close by. One man in each pair had a small machine with him: it looked like a computer game or something. They held the machines in front of them, studying the screens.

It didn't take them long to cover the town. Whatever they were looking for, they didn't find. Within an hour they were back in the main square, looking down towards the harbour. Only one of them was on the phone now. That was when King Boris saw them.

'Oh,' he said thoughtfully. 'Ah. Time to go now.'

Claudio and Younus were still discussing money and supplies, poking about in their wallets and their crates of dates. The Young Lion had chosen his moment, and then slipped invisibly on board Younus's boat, directly into the hold.

'Come along,' said King Boris, an urgency entering his voice that made Claudio look up. 'Now, and quietly.'

Claudio followed the King's gaze and saw the sixteen men in burnooses coming towards them: not Moroccan, not tourists, not holy men. One of them was wearing sunglasses.

'Yes,' said Claudio.

Younus looked up too.

'*Aiwa*,' he said, picking up the last crate of dates. '*Yalla*.'

As the men started asking questions along the seafront, *El Baraka* took off on the tide.

What the Young Lion found in the hold made him yowl.

'What are you doing here!' he screeched as he landed on a pile of soft fur with legs and teeth and whiskers.

'I'm coming too,' said Elsina.

'No, you're not,' said the Young Lion.

'Try and stop me!' she said.

'Get your leg out of my mouth!' he grumbled.

'Well, stop biting my leg,' she retorted.

'Oww! How did you get here?'

'I ran, and I watched, and I used my common sense,' she said. 'I'm not stupid, you know.'

The Young Lion was very angry. His sister had put him in an impossible position. They argued, hissing furiously at each other under their breath, until they heard footsteps approaching and realized that Claudio, Primo and Younus were coming on board.

'And what am I meant to say to the family, when you get killed? Or when we both do, because I have to go and rescue you?' the Young Lion snarled as quietly as he could.

'If we're both killed you won't have a chance to explain, will you?' whispered Elsina crossly. 'Now shut up. I've come to help and I have every right to! Don't be such a pig!'

Then Younus and Claudio were right above them, and the Young Lion was unable to reply for fear of giving himself away. But the moment they moved on, he started hissing at her again. 'You'll be a liability!' he said. 'You'll slow me down and bring danger on us all! And you'd better behave!'

It smelt bad in the hold, but Elsina didn't mind. He couldn't send her back, and in due course he would find out how useful she was.

'I will be an angel among Lionesscubs,' she replied.

'And you'll have to eat fish,' he retorted.

Oh, she thought, remembering the long journey down the Mediterranean. Oh, yuck.

*

Magdalen and Aneba stood side by side on the deck of *Suleiman's Joy*, watching as the sun slowly moved down the scarlet sky in front of them. *Old Yeller* had been a dark dot on the sea ahead of them; now, as the sheet of ocean before them turned to molten gold, it was impossible to pick it out at all. Their eyes dazzled and burned as they stared into the furnace of the late evening. Magdalen blinked. Aneba tried and failed to shade his eyes in such a way that he could make out anything ahead to the west.

'Suleiman,' said Magdalen. 'How will we not lose the other boat in the dark?'

'Darkness exists only for the eye of the body,' said Suleiman. 'The eye of the heart is illuminated by wisdom.'

Magdalen looked at Aneba. Aneba looked at her.

'Oh dear,' he said.

'God will guide us,' said Suleiman, a happy smile on his lips.

'God helps those who help themselves,' murmured Aneba.

'So can you sail?' Magdalen asked him.

'Of course, my love,' he said. 'I can do anything.'

But she noticed that he was watching the crew closely to see what they did, and why. She did the same herself. You never know. Then when Suleiman set up the night watch, when the day's solar power took the boat along on autopilot through the darkness, she went below into the cabin and began to look at the sea charts, and the equipment, and the

books, and to make friends with the sailorguys, and to learn what they knew.

And later that night, as they sat huddled from the Atlantic wind, rocking on the swell, in the cockpit for a bit of privacy, Magdalen said to Aneba, 'The guys on the quay said they were going to the US. But is that really where Maccomo would take him?'

The wind was cold down their necks as they tried to remember everything Charlie had said about Maccomo; everything they knew about him.

Uppermost in their minds was what Maccomo had said that night in Essaouira, in the hotel. Aneba and Magdalen had been hiding behind a screen, believing Mabel still to be loyal to Maccomo, and had heard with their own appalled ears as he outlined his plan to sell the Catspeaking boy to the Corporacy, via Rafi Sadler, and make his fortune . . .

Mabel.

'Ring her,' said Aneba.

Through the rushing waves, in the dark, it was hard to make out what the telephone was doing. Was there still a signal? Would it work out here?

The screen lit up. The number rang, far away.

And Mabel picked up.

'Hi, Magdalen!' she said brightly. 'I'm on the train! You sound like you're in the middle of the sea.'

'I am,' said Magdalen. 'Listen – we might be cut off at any moment. Listen – Maccomo.'

'Yes?' said Mabel, guarded suddenly, warned off by the tone of her sister's voice, and by the subject matter.

'Mabel, if Maccomo got hold of Charlie, what would he do?'

'What?' Mabel said. 'I can't hear you.'

The wind was wheezing, echoing the noises on the phone line.

'IF MACCOMO GOT HOLD OF CHARLIE, WHAT WOULD HE DO WITH HIM?'

'God, I hate to think!' said Mabel in alarm, but luckily Magdalen couldn't make it out, and by the time Mabel spoke again she had realized that wasn't the most tactful thing to say.

'WHAT! WHY? HAS HE?' she shouted instead.

'YES! HE'S GOT HIM ON A SHIP. THEY'RE HEADING OUT TO SEA FROM ESSAOUIRA. WHERE ARE THEY GOING?'

'Oh my god,' breathed Mabel. She felt suddenly as if it were all her fault. As if she should have known, and could have prevented this. The ache in her sister's voice, the courage with which she was sticking to the point despite the pain she must be feeling . . . God, her brave little sister.

'HE WON'T HURT HIM!' she bellowed. 'HE VALUES HIM! CATSPEAKING! WANTS TO LEARN!' She racked her brain. What else?

Her mind too flicked back to the night when Maccomo

had proposed to her. What a fool she had been ever to have cared for him.

'CORPORACY!' she shouted.

'BUT WHERE?' shrieked Magdalen.

Mabel didn't know where. But she knew how high Maccomo was aiming.

'HEADQUARTERS!' she yelled. 'I DON'T KNOW WHERE THAT IS! I CAN TRY AND FIND OUT! ARE YOU ON A SHIP? I'LL TRY AND CALL – I'LL . . . WHAT DO YOU WANT ME TO DO?'

She'd been yelling into a vacuum. The line was dead.

Everyone in the carriage was staring at her.

'She's right,' murmured Magdalen. 'He'll have gone back to plan A. Sell Charlie to the Corporacy.'

'So does that mean Rafi's involved?' said Aneba.

'Well, he was the original contact,' she murmured.

At that moment her phone flashed the message icon.

Charlie's number.

Magdalen and Aneba read it swiftly; looked at each other.

'Go on, call it up,' Aneba said, but Magdalen's hand was shaking so much, she hardly could.

They listened together, their heads touching, leaning in to the telephone.

'In a boat, in a sack,' whispered Magdalen.

'Quick, ring him,' Aneba said.

Magdalen looked up at him. 'What if he's hiding – what

if the ring gives him away? What if they hear and take the phone off him . . .?'

'He said it's on vibrate,' said Aneba. 'Here, I'll do it.'

He dialled his son's number. Held his breath.

Meanwhile, on board *El Baraka*, while Younus and his guys were considering whether to try and catch some dinner, Claudio took the opportunity to look around the boat. It seemed well made and shipshape, but dreadfully small. He peered into the hold and, hearing a noise, swung himself down.

In the corner, he thought he saw a flash.

He went over. Behind a trunk, tucked away . . .

He gasped.

'*Dio mio*, is a Lion,' he whispered. 'Always more Lion!'

And then: 'But Lions don't have six legs,' he said to himself. 'Er – seven . . . er . . . and two tails . . .'

The Young Lion coughed sheepishly.

Elsina raised her sweet face and purred at him.

'Elsina!' he squeaked. 'My beautiful girl!' To tell the truth he was extremely charmed, but charming purring was all very well – what were they going to be fed on? Claudio shook his head furiously, as if by shaking it they might go away.

'How come there is Lions?' he squeaked, trying to squash his outrage. 'I don't have enough to eat for two Lions! How can I feed? How can I hide? *O Dio mio, ma che fate qui, siete pazzi leonacci, è troppo questo, non posso . . .'*

Claudio felt he ought to be cross. He was cross.

But Elsina was so sweet.

'You plan this or what?' Claudio demanded.

The Young Lion looked as affronted as he could. Elsina looked as winning as she could.

Claudio stared at them and it began to sink in to him just what a position he was in.

I should turn straight around and go back to Venice, he thought. This is absurd.

But as absurd as it was, he could not seriously consider deserting Charlie. He just couldn't. And how could he turf these Lions out now?

So, he thought, I'll just be shovelling *merda di leoni* overboard every morning, and the sailors will think I'm completely *pazzo*, and they'll be right. I must find a way to take them in my cabin. More safe.

He and Boris had been given a tiny cabin to share. The Lions would just have to sneak into it, and stay put until – *o Dio mio*. What would King Boris say?

Just then Younus called down into the hold. Putting his finger to his lips to shush the Lions, Claudio turned and slipped out. Younus and King Boris were discussing a simple yet vital question: where were they going?

'We have a clear view of *Suleiman's Joy*,' Younus said excitedly. 'We can catch them if you like. Certainly we won't lose them. But please, it would help to know where

we are going. It's not like New York "Follow That Cab!"
There at least they have streets and back-up other cops in
automobiles coming up vroom vroom bang bang.'

'My dear boy,' said King Boris kindly. 'Let me assure
you that we have not the slightest idea where we are going,
and indeed, as soon as any information reaches us, believe
me, dear boy, you will be the first to know.' And with those
reassuring words, he pit-patted up to the bows, where he
planned to enjoy the magnificent sunset.

The Head Chief Executive thought quietly. None of the
Ashanti family to be found in Essaouira, though they had
been there recently. A Lioncatcher. Three boats heading
west suddenly; two of them following the first. A young
guy with a bad arm asking for a Liontrainer.

So who's on those boats?

Who's following who, and why and . . . where?

He thought. All heading west, following each other.

How interesting.

Rafi Sadler really had made a mess of things, but perhaps . . .

The Head Chief Executive made a decision, and then he
made a call.

Back in Essaouira, the men in burnooses packed up and
left.

CHAPTER
SEVEN

On board *Old Yeller*, just as Charlie felt the unmistakable sound of Maccomo's voice vibrate in his ear, the telephone started to vibrate in his pocket.

He couldn't answer it! Maccomo would take it away, and then how would he communicate? There were no cats in mid-ocean to take notes.

But what was Maccomo doing here? He was meant to be lying in a stupor under a tree at Lionhome! How had he escaped? How had the Lions let him?

A glance at the screen told him that, yes, it was his mother.

He bit his lip. He could hardly bear it. It would go to Message, and she would leave one, and he could call for it later and hear her sweet voice, and her wise advice. But he hated that he couldn't answer and speak to her now.

Maccomo, meanwhile, had taken Rafi's phone off him. Rafi had quite a lot to say about that.

'Excuse *me*, Maccomo, but what exactly is going on 'ere? I came to you *in* good faith, *with* a business proposition, and now you're sticking me in the basement of this bliddy boat like I'm your prisoner, and excuse *me*, trying to take my phone off of me. What's up, man? What's the problem?' You could hear in his voice that he was torn between being really angry and wanting to be threatening and rude, and realizing that actually Maccomo had all the power so he'd be better off sucking up to him. It made for a very nasty mixture.

Charlie found himself listening to Rafi's voice for any kind of family similarity.

'You have no proposition, Rafi,' Maccomo said, turning away from him. 'You have nothing to offer me.'

'Well, I did 'ave!' crowed Rafi. 'I only had your favourite little Catspeaking Charlie bliddy Ashanti, didn't I, back in town? So what all this sweeping off to sea is about, I don't know. We could make a good deal here, Maccomo! I've got the contacts, and the boy . . .'

'If you have so much, Rafi, why do you need me? And why are you sitting tied up like a chicken in the bottom of my boat?' asked Maccomo quietly. 'And why do you lie to me? A man who is succeeding has no need to lie.' His voice was as calm and cool as ever. Maccomo never raised his voice. Charlie remembered the flash of dark fire in the back of Maccomo's eyes, the only way he ever expressed passion. He bet the dark fire was flashing now – just the once. Nothing extravagant.

And Charlie knew too from Maccomo's voice that he

hadn't been taking the medicine drops. This was the clear, calm, dangerous Maccomo of old.

Charlie lay silent in his sack. He longed for Sergei to come to him. And little Ninu!

'We got your message, darling,' Magdalen cried into the telephone. 'We're coming after you. Where are you going?' She closed her eyes, trying to think what was important to say. She couldn't think. 'Love you,' she ended weakly, and rang off.

'Sweetheart,' said Aneba kindly, but at the kindness in his voice she started to weep, and he was not able to speak to her for a moment or two except to murmur comforting words he hardly believed himself. Soon, though, she wiped her nose and shook her head and said, 'Yes?'

'The Corporacy has all these Communities, all over the world,' he said. 'But Mabel said Headquarters and I think she must be right. The Headquarters, I've always heard, is secret.'

'So . . . what?' asked Magdalen.

'They've got Communities in California and New England, and Florida, and in Mexico and Brazil and Venezuela and Chile, in Canada – I remember reading a list . . . But there's one place you don't hear about . . .'

'What?'

'Have you ever heard of a Corporacy Gated Village Community in the Caribbean?'

'Well, no, I haven't.'

'And isn't that odd? Because wouldn't you think they'd have loads down there? What with the climate, and the beaches, and the palm trees, and how lovely it is? Holiday communities, and retirement communities, and all that stuff? But you don't hear about it.'

'It's like the case of the dog that didn't bark,' said Magdalen, perking up.

'Exactly. Why didn't the dog bark? You'd have expected it to bark – it should have barked. Why don't we hear about the Corporacy Communities in the Caribbean – we'd expect to. So there has to be a reason why we don't . . .'

'And you think it's the secrecy.'

'I think it might be.'

Magdalen was silent a moment. She huddled against Aneba.

'Imagine,' she said, 'how Charlie must have felt that first night, running away from Rafi, chasing after us without any idea where we were being taken. The bravery of that boy . . .'

'And here we are, in the same situation,' said Aneba.

Magdalen closed her eyes for a moment.

'We'll tell Suleiman tomorrow,' she said. 'It's all westward anyway, for now. Come on. Let's go in and get some rest.'

*

It had been quite uncomfortable enough trussed up in a dusty sack without the knowledge that Rafi Sadler was just a few metres away from him, or that he had been captured by Maccomo. Now, trussed up in the dusty sack, with his two enemies in the dank hold with him, and his mother's call unanswered in his pocket, his friends all left behind in Morocco, Charlie felt about as low as he could feel.

He hardly dared to breathe – and not just because the dust was setting off his asthma. He was horribly aware of how he had punched Rafi. He was even more horribly aware of how he had handed Maccomo over to the Lions, and left him bound and drugged in the dust. He was utterly confused by the new situation that Rafi was his cousin, and worried about what, if anything, it meant – for example, was he supposed to like him now? Or at least not loathe everything about him? And he was most horribly aware that neither of these two guys was going to forgive him one tiny little bit for his having got the better of them, and made fools of them, and beaten them. Both of them would want to make him suffer. And both of them were much nastier than he was, and would think of much nastier ways to punish him than he had thought of for them.

He was aware that at various stages he could have just let the Lions eat them both, and that if he had done that, he would not be in this situation now.

But it still wouldn't have been right.

Especially not his cousin. Snike it, he didn't want Rafi to be his cousin!

Anyway, why wouldn't it be right? Wouldn't it count as self-defence, given that neither of these two would leave him alone? He wasn't asking them to follow him around and try to steal him the whole time – wouldn't he be justified in whatever he did to get them off his back?

Oh, but what a stupid time to be having an argument with himself. He had no power to defend himself at all now. Here he was in a sack. And if he were let out of the sack, there's no telling if things would get any better. At least now Maccomo was ignoring him and Rafi didn't seem to know he was here. Actually, he'd like to stay in the sack. Much better. Safer.

At that moment Maccomo said a few words in Arabic to the other man, the one who had tried to take Rafi's phone off him.

'Talk bliddy English, won't you?' Charlie heard Rafi say crossly.

And then the other man was manhandling Charlie, pulling the sack off him – pulling his hair in the process.

'Oww,' said Charlie.

'What the crike!' said Rafi.

'You. Here,' said the man, and swiftly lashed Charlie's arms to his chest.

Charlie's limbs were stiff and his eyes blinking even in the gloom of the hold, but despite it all, in that moment he remembered something. A voice from months ago: 'Make your muscles tense and big, and fill your chest and belly with air. Then when you relax and breathe out, the ropes will be looser around you.' He did it. He could feel his torso and biceps swelling. The man was tying Charlie's wrists with the same rope behind his back, and then the other end of the rope to one of the upright struts of the ship, leaving a loose sort of lead of a foot or two.

Charlie tried to focus. The light was dim, the hold was large, a doorway up to the left let in a shaft of light.

Lashed to the opposite strut, some five metres in front of Charlie, stood Rafi.

Rafi let loose a mouthful of extremely bad language.

Charlie held his chest-filling breath.

Maccomo said nothing.

The other man tugged on Charlie's bonds, to make sure they were tight. Charlie still held.

'You! You despicable little snike, you scumbag ratface little piece of . . . I'll have you. I'll bliddy have you, Charlie bliddy snike-face – you little graspole, you . . .'

Charlie let out his breath as gently as he could, and relaxed.

'Yeah, hello to you too, Rafi,' he said with a tired little smile.

Things were now about as bad as they could be.

'SILENCE!' said Maccomo. He stared at them, from one to the other, standing like a judge between them, a dark figure with the lighted doorway behind him. 'You two small boys will not trouble my peace of mind. You will be silent. There has been a nonsensical conception,' he said, his voice growing silky again, 'that what either of you chooses to do has some effect on me – that you have some kind of power, or influence, on me and what I do. This idea is not to be entertained. It is nonsense. You two small boys are little nothings. Remember that. Little nothings. I take no notice of you.'

He turned on his heel as if to leave, his robe swishing behind him on the grubby wooden floor. Then he paused a moment.

'Oh,' he said. 'And should either of you do any harm to the other, the same harm will be done back to him.'

And then he left. His henchman followed him. Charlie wriggled a little. Yes, the bonds were bearable.

Silence filled the dim cavern of the hold. Silence, and the immutable rushing of the sea beyond the wooden body of the ship.

Charlie was relieved. He'd been expecting a huge telling-off, a beating – he didn't know what, but something more than a little run-of-the-mill humiliation. Lord, he could put up with Maccomo being rude to him. That was no problem.

Rafi, though, was furious. He was silent, for the moment, but he was breathing heavily, his eyes were glowing and his face had gone white with anger. Charlie eyed him carefully, trying not to let it show that that was what he was doing.

If Rafi was going to be so very excitable, Charlie would have to be very careful not to set him off by accident, by looking at him, or some other unforgivable insult.

He might set him off on purpose, to amuse himself. But that was something different.

Well, as soon as he was sure Maccomo was out of earshot, Rafi went off anyway – a good ten-minute diatribe about Charlie's stupidity, his ugliness, his weakness, his parents and their stupidity, ugliness and weakness, a brief foray into his pride and thinking himself so special, and how he was no better than anybody else, a comment on his having no friends . . . At first Charlie blocked it out, but of course phrases slipped through, and gradually Charlie realized something rather interesting. All these insults that Rafi was throwing at him were actually true of Rafi himself. It was Rafi who had proved himself to be vain and foolish and proud and weak and stupid and arrogant and greedy and uppity, Rafi whose parents had let him down, Rafi who had no friends. Only the ugliness didn't apply – even Charlie could see that Rafi was very good-looking, with his long eyelashes and high cheekbones. Though actually the effect was ruined by his spoiled and mean expression, and the whole combination, which in a way made him really ugly.

This realization made it easier to hear Rafi's shower of insults. It also had the slightly odd effect of making Charlie feel sorry for Rafi. Imagine knowing so little about yourself! Imagine having to be such a horrible person as Rafi!

But he stopped himself. He'd felt sorry for Rafi before, and he'd learned that being sorry for Rafi just comes up behind you and bites you on the bum, and Rafi being his cousin didn't change that. He wasn't going to be sorry for Rafi and he wasn't going to be sorry for himself.

Charlie sneaked another look at him. Did he and Rafi look at all alike? Did he look like Mabel? For the first time, Charlie wondered who Rafi's dad was.

Stop it, he told himself. He was going to move round to the other side of the strut where he couldn't see Rafi, and he was going to sit down and work out how this terrible situation could have come about, and where they could be going, and what he could do about it.

'Don't you turn away from me, you little runt, you come back here when I'm talking to you, who do you think you are . . .'

Charlie leaned back against the strut, stared at the wall, and tried to think.

As soon as it was dark enough, and the humans mostly asleep, Sergei started sniffing around the boat. It was bigger than he'd expected, but even so it didn't take him long to sniff out where Charlie was being kept. He located two entrances: the door, towards the stern, and a hatch, towards the bow. Both were strong and firmly closed. But that was just human entrances.

Now, he thought. Where's the Rat Network?

Almost all ships — and many other places — have a Rat Network. (The *Circe* didn't, because the rats were put off by the smell of the Lions. They wouldn't go on board if you paid them — and rats will do anything for money.) It didn't take him long to find it: a dingy-looking hole leading from the corridor by the galley, the ship's tiny kitchen. Too small for Sergei, obviously, but the chameleon could do it.

Sergei went back to the coil of rope they were calling home.

'Oi, reptile,' he said cheerfully. 'Got a job for yer.'

Ninu poked his face out. 'Really?' he said. No one had ever asked Ninu to do a job before. He rather liked the idea.

Until he saw the hole, that is.

'I can't go down there!' he squeaked. 'It's dark and horrible! Who lives down there? What if they bite me?'

Sergei sighed theatrically. 'Excuse *me*,' he said. 'If you could manage to overcome your pathetic bourgeois antipathy to the dark and the unknown, you could become, instantly, the hero of the hour by making contact with Charlie, tellin' 'im that we're 'ere, transporting messages and generally in all senses saving the bliddy day. If yer don't, we're stuck. So make yer bliddy mind up, would yer? I'm getting cold sat here.'

Ninu stared. He shivered.

'Whose hole is it?' he asked in a small voice.

'Rats',' said Sergei.

'Oh,' said Ninu.

And he took a tiny breath, and he made his mind up, and he slipped into the hole.

'Bloomin' 'eck,' mused Sergei admiringly. 'I didn't think he'd do it.'

It was dark and smelly in the hole, dusty under Ninu's tummy. He scurried along, trundling like a toy on wheels, hoping that there wouldn't be a fork where he would have to decide which way to go. He smelt air ahead – not fresh air, but the wide air of a large space. He smelt rat too, but old rat, not fresh rat right here about to challenge him and bite him and want to know who he was and what he was doing. He smelt rat from half an hour ago. Rat who might be here next time. But not rat right now, so it was OK. Just.

He scurried on.

There was no light at the end of the tunnel but he could tell when he emerged. The space seemed enormous. Sergei had said Charlie was in here – but where in here?

Ninu stayed close to the wall, and listened carefully.

Under the hard rushing sound of the sea, two lots of breathing. One over there, one over here. Ninu waited. His eyes had adjusted to the dark (chameleons see much better than most lizards, and they are the only reptile that can focus on one spot). But he couldn't see which person was Charlie, and he didn't at all want to approach any person who was not Charlie.

He waited.

And he waited.

(Up in the corridor Sergei waited too, in a state of increasing agitation.)

And he waited some more.

He was not a reptile for nothing. Nobody can wait like a reptile.

After an hour and a half, one of the sets of breathing rolled its head and muttered the words, 'Sergei, you idiot . . .'

Ninu zipped across the floor to the source of the sound, and gently with his little fingers he took hold of Charlie's thumb and squeezed.

Charlie woke in confusion, from very deep sleep. But he had spent enough time in trouble to keep his mouth shut in moments of confusion. He blinked and stared at the thumb that was being pinched. As his vision settled, he took in the sight of Ninu, pale in the darkness, his huge eyes rolling, and his face in a grin.

'Ninu!' Charlie whispered delightedly. 'Ninu!' He kept his voice as tiny as he could but his pleasure was immense and almost burst out. 'What are you doing here? Fantastic!' He put his face close to the chameleon and automatically spoke in Cat, because he was talking to an animal. 'Fantastic!' he whispered again. Ninu gave him two little squeezes more, and crept up on to his hand.

'Sergei is upstairs,' said Ninu quietly. 'We jumped on

board when you were grabbed. Sergei told your friend from Venice, and he was going to tell your parents, and everybody is telling everybody. Everybody is chasing you!'

Charlie's grin was as wide as it could be. Then he realized what he'd heard. 'What friend from Venice?' he asked.

'A tall blond person,' said Ninu. 'Talks Italian. His name is . . .' But Ninu couldn't remember the name.

'Claudio?' said Charlie, bewildered.

'Yes!' Ninu replied. 'Claudio. I met him in the café after you'd gone ahead. Very nice. Asking about you. Then Sergei rushed up saying the Lioncatcher had pushed you into a trolley, and we all rushed down to the quay and Sergei and I ended up on the boat and Claudio was still on the shore.'

Charlie was confused by this. What was Claudio doing in Essaouira? He was supposed to be in Venice, looking after Primo.

'Did you hear any news of the Lions, Ninu?' Charlie asked. 'Because the guy in charge of pushing me into the trolley is Maccomo, the Liontrainer, and he was the Lions' prisoner. He's escaped – he's on this boat now. But I don't know if the Lions are all right.'

Charlie couldn't imagine how the Lions could have let Maccomo escape. Unless – had someone come with guns?

He didn't want to think about it.

But however it had happened, it was true: Maccomo was free.

'No news of Lions,' said Ninu sadly. 'But no bad news

of Lions either. So that's good.' He rolled one eye over towards the other sleeping shape. 'Who's that?'

'Oh dear, Ninu,' whispered Charlie. 'It's all a very long story that you've got yourself involved in here. It's not quite the jolly overland trip to Ghana I mentioned.'

'Plenty of insects on a boat,' said Ninu. 'I don't mind. Who *is* that?'

'That's my cousin,' said Charlie.

'Nice!' said Ninu.

'Well,' said Charlie, 'he's also the guy who took my parents in the first place . . .' Quietly he told Ninu the story.

By the end Ninu looked quite shocked – at least, Charlie thought he did, but it's hard to read a chameleon's expression under the best of circumstances. Also Ninu always looked a bit shocked, with his frilled head and bug eyes.

'So now Maccomo has kidnapped both of you?' he asked.

'Yup,' said Charlie.

'I'd better tell Sergei,' said Ninu.

'Can he come down here?' Charlie asked keenly. He longed for his friend's sarky good sense and also, although Sergei was not at all a cuddly cat, he would sometimes lean against Charlie's leg in a way that was both warm and comforting, and Charlie could really do with some of that now.

'Too big,' said Ninu. 'Only I am small enough to go down the rat holes.'

'Ninu,' said Charlie. 'Did you go down a rat hole?'

'Yes,' said Ninu proudly, very glad now that he had.

'Thank you,' said Charlie, from the bottom of his heart.

Across the room, Rafi stirred in his sleep.

'Ninu,' whispered Charlie, 'go back to Sergei and tell him I'm really, really glad you're both here. Tell him I've rung both my parents and my mum's rung back but I haven't been able to talk to her yet.' (He said 'yet', but in his heart he feared he would not be able to now: he had heard her message and taken comfort from it, but his phone had no signal and they were getting further from land all the time. He hadn't let himself think about how sad this made him.) 'Tell him Rafi's here. Tell him I'm pretty sure Maccomo must be taking both of us to the Corporacy – after all, he was thinking of selling me to them before, and Rafi was working for them but kept getting everything wrong. Tell him to think about where a Corporacy place might be. Ask him if he can keep an eye on what direction we're travelling, and –' Charlie was thinking quickly – 'see if he can eavesdrop at all, pick up any information from the humans on board. Ask him to find out who is on board, how many, where they are, what they do . . .'

'All right,' said Ninu.

'Sorry,' said Charlie. 'Getting a bit carried away. I am so glad you're here. Come back again soon.' And Ninu squeezed his finger again, and scuttled bravely back up the rat hole.

And then Rafi's voice came from across the hold.

'So who's yer friend? Some bliddy cat? Can't you get

him to go and do something useful, like bite Maccomo's neck for us so he bleeds to death in his sleep, instead of waking me up in the middle of the night with your chatting? It's hard enough to sleep here, for crike sake.'

Drat.

Well, at least he hadn't understood what they were saying.

It *was* hard to sleep.

But Charlie's friends were here and, despite everything, that made him happy.

The sack he had been stuffed in had been abandoned nearby, so he reached out for it with his foot, rolled it into a makeshift pillow, and curled himself up. Sergei and Ninu. Claudio! Mum and Dad . . . He wasn't alone.

CHAPTER
EIGHT

So it was that the *Old Yeller* sailed westward across the Atlantic, and *Suleiman's Joy* followed her, and *El Baraka* followed *Suleiman's Joy*.

Or so it was, until about four o'clock that morning, when *Old Yeller* changed course for the south, and nobody aboard *Suleiman's Joy* could see that she had, so *Suleiman's Joy* continued westward across the Atlantic, and *El Baraka* continued to follow *Suleiman's Joy*, and Charlie was, after all, more alone than he thought.

After sundown, Charlie was eating a bowl of rather unpleasant slop, his back still turned to Rafi.

'Bliddy 'orrible bliddy food,' Rafi sneered bad-temperedly. 'This is probably like what your mum makes, eh, Charlie?'

'Yeah, exactly,' Charlie replied cheerfully. 'Boiled worms is her best, with slug sauce. You should come over one time and try it, when we're back home. You'd probably love it.'

'I don't go round visiting for little tea parties, Charlie

Dumbhead,' said Rafi wearily.

'No, of course you don't – no one invites you, do they? Cos you've got no friends, have you, Rafi?' Charlie responded. 'Rafi No-mates, Rafi Never-had-no-mates . . .'

Underneath the banter, however, was something strange. Charlie had, for example, nearly said, 'Yeah, well, at least I have a mum'; or 'At least I know who my mum is'; or 'You don't even know who your mum is – and I do!' Danger lurked in every swapped insult, but of one thing Charlie was sure. He did *not* want Rafi knowing that they were related. So, he had to guard his words, watch his lip, keep his trap shut under provocation.

Later, Ninu appeared, with the news that they were heading south.

'Down the coast of Africa,' Charlie mused to Ninu. 'Where can we be going?'

'I can tell you!' squeaked the little creature, full of pride. 'Sergei overheard the sailors talking. They are going to –' and here he took a breath and concentrated hard, because he wanted to get it right – 'A krar.'

'A krar?' said Charlie, mystified. 'What . . .? Accra! But – oh, that's good news, that's really good.'

Accra was the capital of Ghana. Accra was where Aneba came from. Accra was where Grandma lived! Charlie had friends and family, aunts and uncles – Accra was where he and his parents had been planning to go anyway! Accra was just the place to jump ship!

'But why?' he asked suddenly. 'Why is Maccomo going to Accra?'

'Sergei says,' said Ninu carefully, 'that they're not staying there. They have to pick something up, then they're heading on somewhere else.'

'Then tell Sergei that we must make a plan to jump ship at Accra,' whispered Charlie. 'However we can do it. I can't risk trying to get out of here before we get there, so it's up to you. You and Sergei must think of something.'

Ninu smiled his long, flat smile. 'OK,' he said, and he ran up Charlie's arm and rubbed his head on Charlie's chin, which was the only bit he could reach. 'Don't worry. We'll make a brilliant plan.'

Charlie spent the rest of the evening practising his Twi under his breath. Accra!

On board *Suleiman's Joy*, Magdalen and Aneba were quietly frustrated. When they had woken from a scrappy night's sleep, there had been no sign of *Old Yeller* in front of them. They went to see Suleiman, but he said it didn't matter, God led and man followed, and such was the way of the virtuous man.

'So what do we do now?' asked Aneba, peering through Suleiman's telescope.

'We carry on,' said Magdalen. 'I really think we have no choice. We'll carry on, and we'll catch up with them.'

'Talking of which,' said Aneba, handing the telescope

over, 'have you noticed the ship behind us? I spotted it last night, and it's still with us.'

Magdalen looked. Yes, there was a dot far behind them. 'Is it following us?' she asked.

'Well, I think so,' he mused. 'Suleiman?'

Suleiman observed that many men followed the same path, yet each man's path is his own. At this Aneba buried his face in his hands, whether to laugh or to weep Magdalen couldn't tell. Suleiman relented: 'She is a ship from Essaouira,' he said. 'She has been with us since we left, and she is with us now. It is not for me to know why.'

'Claudio?' suggested Magdalen.

'That would be nice,' her husband said. 'That would be great.'

Things were not going well on board *El Baraka*. Younus very much wanted to catch up with Suleiman, overtake him, shout things over the rails – what, he hadn't quite thought, but something dashing. And he still wanted to know where they were going.

'Your question is not unreasonable,' said King Boris politely. 'And may I assure you that if I knew, I would tell you. But I don't. Nor does Claudio. So we must come follow, follow, follow, follow, follow, follow them, whither shall we follow, follow, follow, whither shall we follow, follow them? To the greenwood, to the greenwood, to-oo-oo the greenwood, greenwood tree . . .'

To the Greenwood

TRADITIONAL.

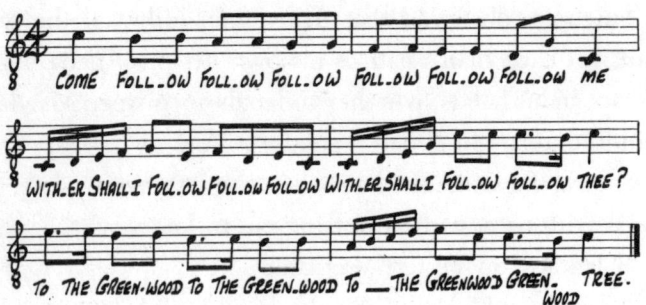

COME FOLL..OW FOLL..OW FOLL..OW FOLL..OW FOLL..OW FOLL..OW ME

WITH..ER SHALL I FOLL..OW FOLL..OW FOLL..OW WITH..ER SHALL I FOLL..OW FOLL..OW THEE?

TO THE GREEN..WOOD TO THE GREEN..WOOD TO —THE GREENWOOD GREEN.. TREE.
WOOD

He had started singing.

'What?' said Younus.

'What?' said Claudio.

What? wondered Elsina and the Young Lion, as they lay in Claudio and King Boris's cabin, into which they had snuck in the dead of night, and hidden under a blanket.

Younus sighed. 'Please,' he said. 'When you know, can you tell me?'

Claudio was more worried. How was he going to tell King Boris that there were two Lions in his hammock?

Seven days later, Sergei saw something most extraordinary through the ship's rail.

The day was calm, and the sea lay like a great dark mirror. The sailors, melting slightly in the southern heat, were snoozing while the solar-powered autopilot drove the ship onward. Maccomo, in the cabin, was brooding. Charlie was counting to a hundred and back again, in Twi. Rafi was gnawing his nails, having dreadful nightmares about what was going to be done to him. And Sergei was lying, as usual, in the shade of a lifeboat on deck, catching a light breeze and enjoying the generally fishy smell of *Old Yeller*. As he lay he mused quietly on how to manufacture some kind of safe shipwreck from which Charlie, Ninu and he could safely and swiftly escape, while everybody else either drowned (Maccomo and Majid) or were held up so long that they couldn't possibly get in Charlie and Sergei's way. It was a tall order, and Sergei wasn't sure he could pull it off.

And then he saw the extraordinary thing.

It was a fountain, in the middle of the otherwise rather calm sea. It just appeared, beside him. He opened one eye, saw it, blinked, and then jumped up in a muffled squawk when it squirted him.

He stared.

It was moving away from the ship.

Cautiously, Sergei peeked over the edge.

It was coming back.

He stepped back and looked swiftly around to see if anyone else had noticed. They hadn't. Then he stepped forward again, because he couldn't resist it. What *was* this?

The fountain disappeared.

In its place was an enormous . . .

Well, it looked a bit like an eye.

'I think it's an eye,' whispered Ninu, from between Sergei's knees.

'Whose eye?' whispered Sergei.

It disappeared again, sinking slowly downward.

Together, bravely, Sergei and Ninu peered over the edge, just in time to see a great dark shadow slip under the water.

'I know what it is!' cried Ninu. 'I have seen her before, in the ocean beyond Essaouira! She is the water-fountain-giant-not-fish! Her name is Madame Baleine! She's – she's a whale!'

And he started to make a curious keening sound, a sort of whistling creaking wailing – the kind of sound, indeed, that whales make when they sing to each other in the depths of the ocean.

Madame Baleine stopped sinking. She rose up.

She was enormous – even the amount of her that they could see was enormous. She looked like a gigantic aubergine, gleaming and dark and smooth. Sergei backed away a little nervously.

She too was singing.

Ninu raised his tiny voice in whale song.

She was answering.

Ninu broke for a second to listen.

'She thinks it's the boat singing to her!' he whispered to Sergei.

Sergei's head whipped up. 'Oh does she?' he murmured, thinking quickly. 'Oh *does* she? Well, keep chattin' with her while I think.'

This had to be useful. A whale!

'What are you tellin' her?' he hissed to Ninu.

'She wanted to know why my voice is so tiny although I am quite a big boat. I told her it's because there is a frog in my throat,' whispered Ninu.

'Oh, for crike sake,' said Sergei, but then he stopped. 'OK,' he said. 'Does she like you?'

'She thinks I'm very strong and handsome,' said Ninu, stifling a giggle.

'My word,' said Sergei. 'Steady on, or you'll 'ave yerself a girlfriend.'

Ninu started to go green at the idea.

'Stay brown!' hissed Sergei. 'You don't want her seein' that yer a tiddly little reptile. Now listen.'

Ninu continued to whistle and keen, but he was listening.

'Tell her – tell her that when we get in near land, near the harbour, you'll need a big slap on the back to clear yer throat. Can you tell her that? Ask her if she'll give you a big wallop.'

'Okey-doke,' said Ninu.

'Not yet!' hissed Sergei. 'When we're close enough in to land.'

Ninu stopped for a moment. 'Sergei,' he said. 'You are really, really clever.'

Sergei smiled in his ratty whiskers. 'Well, it's a less than transcendently perfect plan, but it might do.'

Ninu started to sing again. He sang and clicked and whistled, and the whale sang back, and before the sailors had woken from their siestas Ninu's new girlfriend had promised that she would indeed come and give him a big thwack, just as soon as they were near the harbour.

Meanwhile, miles away in the Mediterranean, another ship was sailing. The beautiful *Circe*, with her Circus on board, had come down from Paris, reclaimed her masts at Port St Louis and headed out to sea. On board Mabel was sitting in Major Tib's elegant cabin deep in conversation with him. She was telling him almost everything. He was fascinated and rather cross.

'That boy!' he said. 'That boy! I shoulda just throwed him overboard in the first place like I said. Pirouette! Somebody get Pirouette in here.'

The tough trapeze artiste was with them in moments, wearing her practice clothes, and slightly out of breath.

'Pirouette,' said Major Tib. 'That boy Charlie, that Lionboy . . .'

'Yes?' said Pirouette.

'Mabel here says he took Maccomo's Lions, and that they all went to Africa — whaddaya make a-that?'

'Very laklee,' said Pirouette. 'He's a brave boy.'

'Says he found his parents again all right, in Morocco someplace, and says – says now he's disappeared, and maybe Maccomo has taken him.'

'Maccomo would be very angry. Of course.'

Major Tib was shaking his head. 'That Maccomo! That boy! No respect for the show, either of 'em . . . How 'bout you, Mabel? You headin' off on a wild goose chase too?'

'No,' said Mabel. 'I'm sticking around.'

'Good,' said Major Tib. 'Go and see to your tigers then. Your tigergirl's proved to be highly reliable, but they all missed ya.'

Mabel and Pirouette left together. Both of them were thinking about Charlie.

Maccomo, standing beside Capitaine Drutzel on the deck of *Old Yeller*, was thinking about Mabel. How he had lost her again in Essaouira, how much he loved her, how he would find her again as soon as he had dealt with these stupid boys. Where would they live together, when they were married?

He gazed across the still, calm sea, as the ship creaked east towards the Gold Coast, and Accra. As soon as they were within reception distance of the shore, he would call the Corporacy Headquarters – from Rafi's telephone – and have a word with whoever it was Rafi had been dealing with. Explain how the situation had changed.

Maccomo knew for sure that the Corporacy wanted Charlie. He knew they'd be glad to have Rafi, who had let them down. And he was pretty sure they'd be interested in the other material he'd been offered in Accra too. But he'd like to run it by them. Find out how much they were willing to pay. If it was enough, he might be able to go back for Mabel even sooner than he had hoped.

He looked across at the coast of West Africa, flat and green in the distance. It wouldn't be long now.

Ninu was back in the Rat Network. He and Sergei had agreed that he would go and explain to Charlie what was happening, and stay down there with Charlie for safety's sake – hide in his pocket or something. Sergei would fend for himself and head for the coast, and they'd find each other on shore. Ninu felt very brave and cool now, scurrying along the dark underdeck byways, the tiny tunnels and dusty crevices, doing important deeds, fearless.

Until he saw the rat.

He'd been up and down the network many times since that first time, and he had never seen a rat. He'd been beginning to think they'd deserted, that it was an old network. But then he saw her.

She was very big. Her teeth were yellow and sharp. Her breath was smelly. Her tail was like a long scaly worm. Ninu froze.

'You're in the wrong place, my son,' she said lazily. 'No call for no reptile to be down here. You might get in trouble.'

Ninu was so terrified, he couldn't move. He couldn't speak. His little heart was pitter-pattering and his skin was fading to grey.

'You might get eaten,' she said. 'You got a soft under-belly tucked away under all them scales? I might eat you. You might taste very nice.' Her pointy teeth suddenly seemed to lengthen as she grinned.

'No,' stuttered Ninu. 'Taste horrible. No flavour.'

The rat looked surprised. She wasn't accustomed to her potential dinner addressing her in Rat.

'Not much meat,' said Ninu bravely.

'Oh?' she said.

'Anyway,' said Ninu, his thoughts flailing around, looking for something to divert her. 'Anyway, I can help you.'

'Oh?' she said again.

'Bring you food,' he said. 'Dead food. Much easier.'

'That'd be nice,' she said.

'And,' said Ninu, inspiration striking him, 'I can tell you a secret – if I tell you a very important secret, will you promise not to eat me?'

'What's promise?' said the rat.

'Say something, and then stick to it. Do what you say,' said Ninu.

The rat looked a bit amused by this notion.

'Why'd I want to do that?' she said.

'Loyalty,' said Ninu. 'We'd trust each other and be on each other's side.'

The rat laughed aloud – a nasty sniggering sound.

'I'm a rat,' she said. 'You're welcome to trust me if you want.' And sniggered again.

But Ninu, being an innocent creature, took her at face value.

'Great,' he said. 'Well, listen. This ship is going to be wrecked. Quite soon. It's probably going to sink . . .'

'Sink!' squawked the rat. 'Sink! I'll be off then – excuse me . . . got to get the others . . .'

'Before you go, you should eat!' Ninu squeaked desperately. He had had another brilliant idea. 'Follow me and I'll show you. Really good food. You don't know when you'll be eating again . . .'

The rat hesitated.

'Just down here,' said Ninu invitingly.

He turned to head along the network towards the hold.

'There's humans down that way,' said the rat.

'They can't hurt you,' said Ninu. 'They're tied up. With really juicy fresh rope.'

Rope! The rat's nose quivered. She loved rope. So chewy and flavoursome, and the sailors always kept it locked away from her.

'All right,' she said.

*

Charlie was snoozing. He was woken by a snuffly, nibbly sensation around his hands, an unsettling whiskery feeling, and a sudden release when the rope that had been binding him fell from his wrists.

'What the –?' he cried, but then Ninu was there, grinning his reptile grin and looking amazingly pleased with himself.

Charlie rubbed his wrists and cautiously swung his arms. The rat leapt away. 'Oi,' she muttered, but Charlie didn't notice and Ninu ignored her. He had a plan to explain.

Charlie, glad as he was to be untied, was not reassured by what Ninu had to say.

Outside, the sea was roughening up as the ship came nearer to land. In the dank hold Charlie could feel the sway and pitch of the ship clearly. It was all very well Ninu explaining how they were off the coast of Ghana now, and how close to land they would be before the whale tipped the ship with her great whacking tail. Charlie could envisage all too well the great long Atlantic waves rolling in endlessly on the wide beaches. Charlie knew those waves and beaches: the strong, implacable undercurrents, the dangers awaiting ignorant cheerful swimmers who mistook the palm trees and golden sands for a sign that a holiday mood could prevail; the undertow that ripped your feet from beneath you and sent you hurtling head over heels as it winded you and dragged you down, down under the water and out to sea.

Charlie hadn't particularly liked his last shipwreck. He would've thought Sergei hadn't liked it either.

'Well,' he said.

But Ninu seemed so pleased and proud of the plan that Charlie didn't want to discourage him. Plus, how could they attract the whale back, if they wanted to change the plan? Plus, he had no other plan.

'Well,' he said again. 'Do we know when she's going to do it?'

'Not really,' said Ninu. 'When we're closer in.'

'So at any stage,' Charlie mused, 'this boat could just be flipped.'

'Er, yes,' said Ninu.

'Right,' said Charlie. He took a deep breath, as if more breath taken now would give him more later, when he was going to need it.

He glanced across at Rafi, his head slumped, still tied to his pole. In his mind Charlie saw crashing waters, flying timbers, a helpless human body – with his family blood in it – trying to fight to the surface, but tied. Fighting, fighting to get to the surface, to the air . . .

He closed his eyes. The image persisted.

He breathed deeply again. Charlie had had experience of gasping for breath, when his asthma was bad. But drowning . . . ugh.

'I can't do it,' he murmured.

'Can't do what?' asked Ninu anxiously.

'I can't leave him to drown, tied up,' Charlie replied. 'I can't leave him without a chance.'

And at that moment, a great blow hit the ship – a mighty thwack from underneath that seemed to lift the hull right up out of the water, where it hung for a second, suspended, before crashing mightily back down on to the waves in a big boat bellyflop.

Charlie was knocked to the ground by the first thwack, and then by the thwack of the ship hitting the sea again. But at least he'd been expecting it, so he was able to pull himself up swiftly. Ninu scrambled quickly into his pocket.

Rafi, on the other hand, who had been snoozing, woke with a manic start, and yelled as his hands were viciously jerked against their ropes.

'Rafi,' called Charlie.

Rafi stared up at him. His face was pale, his eyes scared.

'What's happening, man?' he cried in confusion.

Charlie bit his lip. A shudder was running through the very timbers of the ship.

'Stick out your hands,' Charlie said, and Rafi did so, like an obedient child.

'I never want to see you again, Rafi,' Charlie said. And as quickly as he could, he untied Rafi's bonds.

Rafi stared in disbelief.

'We're to be wrecked,' Charlie said. 'Go and break down that door so we don't all drown.'

Rafi didn't need to be told twice. His arms free, he

hurled himself against the cabin door and had it down in three blows. Charlie was first through. As he dashed towards the ladder leading up to the deck, he turned again to Rafi.

'Never again, you hear me?'

Rafi nodded quickly.

And then they were both off, in different directions, their feet skittering and their blood pounding as the ship beneath them lurched violently from the whale's whipcracking blow.

Madame Baleine surveyed her potential new boyfriend. He wasn't very graceful, the way he had landed – plop! – on the waves, and now he was lurching to and fro, trying to get his balance back in the water. He still looked sweet to her, though.

She wondered if the thwack had cleared his throat for him.

Perhaps she should give him another, to make sure.

Up on deck, a jumbled flurry of images greeted Charlie, dazzled as he was by the sunlight and the hugeness of the sky and the sea. The tropical sun was blinding. To port, in the hazy distance, he could make out the white form of a castle rising from the frondy green palms along the coast. Was it Ghana? His heart lifted at the thought. A handful of gleaming towers caught the evening sun, flashing like animal eyes in the distance. Was that Accra? He had no time to look – closer and more immediate were the long waves, the great grey Atlantic, the huge power of the sea, and the decks of *Old Yeller* rising at a peculiar angle. Everything was at a diagonal to him: the deck, the cabins, the mast. In a moment, it was all diagonal the other way and his feet were slipping from beneath him.

To his left, a bunch of sailors were shouting and pointing. Charlie, his eyes alert for Maccomo, slipped over to where they were, clutching at rigging to support himself and very aware of the noise of the boat beneath him. At any moment it could just slip down, down and away . . .

They were pointing at a great dark shape rising in the waves. Charlie stared. It looked like a zeppelin, or a great fat torpedo, and lying spreadeagled along its back was what looked like a drowned scrap of fur, holding on with all its might, its claws dug into the tough, unfeeling hide . . .

It was the whale, and Sergei was riding it!

Here goes, thought Charlie, and with a mighty roar he burst through the crowd of sailors . . .

His intention was to leap over the edge of the boat and land magnificently on the whale's back before riding her in glory across the streaming ocean into his grandmother's arms.

His reality was to be grabbed by five burly sailors and pushed to the deck, where he grazed his cheekbone, banged his knee and bit his tongue.

His view was obscured by a large rough canvas-clad thigh,

Old Yeller &
Madame Baleine

so he didn't see Madame Baleine turn to stream away
without him, nor the flip of her great fluke, which knocked
all the sailors on top of him. A wave slapped up over the
whole pile of them, cold and wet. Strangely, Charlie felt
the heat of the sun on the top of his head even as the cold
sea water soaked him.

The ship began to settle. She was not going to sink this
time after all. The sailors, relieved, organized themselves
and pinned Charlie down, flat on his back, one on each
limb. He was able to look over to the land, not so far away
from them. It looked green and inviting, the treetops waving
gently. Charlie thought about his grandma, how he'd have
showered in her backyard and washed off the smell of that
stinky ship. He thought about her delicious soup and fufu.
He could almost smell the smoky flavour of her shitoh
pepper paste, which he would not now be tasting.

His cheek was stinging where it had been bashed, and
the sailors were heavy as they pinned him down, then rough
when they pulled him up to his feet. He wasn't sure he
could bear this failure. Then, as the sailors manhandled him,
he was able to reach briefly into his pocket.

Deep inside, a tiny reptile hand clasped his finger.

He would bear it. What choice did he have? He would,
he would, he would.

CHAPTER NINE

Maccomo was furious. He had a large, ugly cut across the bridge of his nose, which was still bleeding. Some of the blood had dripped on to his white chemise.

Capitaine Drutzel was scurrying behind him. The capitaine was angry too. He had no idea why on earth a whale would appear out of nowhere, and wallop his ship twice, terrifying the crew and allowing the important prisoners to attempt escape in the chaos.

'The whale has gone just as quickly as it appeared,' he was telling Maccomo. '*Alhamdu lillah*. Another blow like that and *Old Yeller* might have been holed. We must go ashore here, to check the fabric of the ship. If nothing is wrong, it will take a day. If something is wrong, longer. It depends what.'

Maccomo grunted, then produced one of his little black cigarettes. He lit it, squinting at the tip as if it were his enemy.

A sailor appeared at Capitaine Drutzel's side. 'No major damage below, sir,' he said. 'Things knocked about but nothing structural and no leaks as far as we can see.'

Maccomo drew on his cigarette, and turned to see two groups of sailors approaching him. One held Charlie in a full nelson, the other Rafi.

Maccomo's face was pale and cold. He ignored Rafi and addressed himself to Charlie.

'My ship,' he said calmly, 'has been assaulted by a whale.'

He let the sentence hang.

'Do you know why, Charlie?'

Charlie said nothing. If Maccomo wanted to put on a big act, if it made him feel better, that was none of Charlie's business. All that concerned Charlie was that one escape attempt had failed, so he'd better start thinking up another one.

'And how did you get out of the hold?' he asked.

'They were untied, sir. Both of them,' said a sailor.

'Untied!' said Maccomo. 'Both of them! Rafi untied, and Charlie! How can this be? Were you helping each other? How touching.' He stared at them hard, then said, 'Well, it makes no difference. Rafi is going back to the hold in chains with a constant guard, and *you*, Charlie, are going everywhere I go.'

He nodded to one of the sailors, who produced a pair of handcuffs and snapped them round Charlie's wrists behind his back. And a thick band of cloth, which he tied over Charlie's eyes. As Charlie was received into the darkness, the last thing he saw was Rafi's face, his fancy beard grown out into messy stubble, and his sneering eyes filled with fear.

'*Yalla*,' said Maccomo, and the sailor's strong arm snaked round Charlie's elbows again. 'Let's go. Bring him.'

Charlie could sense Maccomo as he passed by him. Maccomo paused, and whispered in Charlie's ear. 'You've given me too much trouble,' he murmured. 'Enough.' And, as he moved on, he cracked the back of Charlie's head hard with his arm, hard enough to knock him to the floor.

Later, Maccomo made a telephone call, shielding his mouth so that Charlie could not overhear his conversation.

'How is my cargo?' he said softly, in French.

A voice in French told him that all was as it should be: the cargo had arrived at the resort, and packaging was scheduled for that evening with shipment to Accra as arranged.

'Change of plan,' Maccomo murmured. 'Ship to Elmina instead. Be in touch constantly. I may have to rearrange.'

Charlie was quiet and obedient. The darkness surrounded him; the heat seeped into him. Maccomo was not literally keeping him in sight all the time, but the sailor never let go of Charlie's elbows, behind his back. He walked when he was prodded, stopped when he was jerked to a stop. He sat when he was pushed to the floor. He said nothing.

After a while it became apparent that they were going ashore. First he was tumbled from *Old Yeller* down into a smaller boat – long and narrow, he could tell because his knees could touch both sides when he spread them. His fingers reached out to touch: the wood of the seat was rough. Was it a Ghanaian fishing canoe – one carved from a single tree trunk, painted in bright colours, bearing a slogan like 'Sea Never Dry' or 'To Yet Not'?

After a journey of lurch and spray, the boat crunched on to land. He could smell it before he sensed beneath his feet the change from the ever-shifting timbers of a ship at sea to the firm ground of Mother Earth. He smelt a smoky, fishy smell, floating on the air, mixing with the cooler breeze from the sea.

The smell filled his heart with longing. This *must* be Ghana, he thought. He trailed his fingers along the canoe as he was bundled out – yes, painted. He breathed deep, picturing eyes and biblical verses painted on the canoe, tall palms, and beyond them rows of round fish kilns with their layers of palm fronds and the fish laid out under the hot sun, above the hot fire, the women tending and turning them. He could almost taste the sweet pungent flavour of smoked fish . . . Charlie remembered his grandmother's low white house, with the frangipani tree outside – it was grey all over, branches like the neck of a dinosaur, and then suddenly out of the grey reptilian bark burst the most beautiful flowers, waxy and soft, the melting colours of sunset, and smelling like heaven. He remembered the red earth of the street outside, the tall, tatty palm trees, and the bald-headed vultures who lived on Auntie Comfort's roof across the way. Grandma used to make fufu and soup, and would send a neighbour's boy to get kelewele — crunchy deep-fried plantains — from the kelewele lady on the corner by the Love of God Grinding Spot, because it was Charlie's favourite. He remembered the smoky, fishy, peppery, homey smell . . .

Around him, people were talking. Maccomo and the sailors were speaking Arabic; and beyond that — well, the voices that chattered of fish prices, the weather and the attractiveness of somebody's new skirt weren't speaking Twi like they do in Accra, but it was pretty similar. Similar enough for Charlie to understand most of it. A different Akan dialect.

Charlie smiled. This wasn't Accra, but it was Ghana all right — somewhere west probably, on the coast, with a castle. He searched his memory. Cape Coast? Elmina?

He was steered away from the voices, then for a while he was left in a shaded spot, alone with the sailor still holding him by the arms. Charlie wondered whether this was the moment to run — but his sense of the man guarding him was that he was big. And the blindfold was tight. And so were the handcuffs. And so was the sailor's grip.

While Capitaine Drutzel located a boatyard, Maccomo strode the seafront with Majid the Lioncatcher. This was not a big town, and it was dominated by its castle: a large, old, white building, with high, thick walls, and deep, shaded doorways. It was right on the beach, as long as a city block, surrounded by sand and rock, with a few palm trees waving their green fronds against the stark salty whiteness of the walls. Inside was a wide, bare courtyard, into which the tropical sun beat down. It was in many ways a handsome building. Or would have been if you didn't know what it was.

Maccomo looked up at it and narrowed his eyes. The end of the building where he was standing was in good condition, but way down the end towards the rocks and the sea the white paint was stained and peeling off, and the window frames were warped. It looked like an old old shell worn down by salt and wind. There was rubbish blowing against the wall, and in contrast to the bustling crowd up here, there was nobody about.

Bad spirits, he thought to himself. Then: 'Come, Majid,' he said. 'Let's take a look. I think this might do for our delivery.'

Charlie sat. The heat sat on top of him. Sweat was trickling down his back and forehead. He wondered where Sergei was.

After a while, Maccomo returned.

'*Yalla*,' he said again shortly. He sounded pleased with himself.

Afterwards Charlie knew exactly when it was that he panicked and started to scream.

He remembered the sailor hoicking him to his feet. He remembered walking along the uneven sand and rocks, in and out of shade. He remembered nearly tripping over something tangly – an old plastic bag, he thought. He remembered moving into full shade, still warm, damp. Some rattling. The rusty sound of a bolt, metal on metal. The shove that pushed him from outside to inside. The tiny doorway, thick walls as he shouldered between them in the narrow space. The sailor's body behind him. And in front of him . . .

A darker darkness. A high ceiling. A dankness. Dark, warm, damp.

And a smell.

A little like urine, a little like sweat, a little like metal. Not strong. Thin. Bitter. Animal. Damp. Old, old, old.

Charlie's nostrils curled, his stomach heaved, his brain remembered, and he began to wail.

He wailed because he knew.

Charlie knew because his parents had told him; because he'd been taken to visit one as a kid. (It had been converted into a museum. He'd blocked his ears and thought resolutely instead about a pop star he liked.) There were twenty-one of them along the coast here. Once there had been eighty. They were forts – built by Europeans hundreds of years ago as storage places for the ivory and gold and spices they were buying, and to protect the lands they were claiming as their own. And later, the storage houses had become slave forts.

It was in these buildings – in *this* building – that the men and women and children captured or bought inland had been stored like goods, packed in until their *owners* were ready to ship them off to be sold in the New World. The captured people had been brought in on the land side, and they had been taken out directly on to the slave ships waiting for them in the sea. Millions of them. It was here that their freedom was destroyed, their past was lost, here that families were broken, sicknesses spread, hopes – and people – killed. Someone catches you, steals you, and suddenly *you* are a slave.

Charlie knew where he was. He knew what had happened here.

Even the stones of this building knew it. The smell of human pain and fear was in every shadow.

And Charlie wailed.

He wailed so loud, the sailor put his hand over his mouth. Charlie bit him like a mad dog, and wailed more. The sailor swore, stood on Charlie's leg to secure him, and ripped the blindfold off him to wrap it over his mouth instead.

Suddenly struck dumb, with this foul-tasting cloth in his mouth, Charlie stood in the dark, panting and heaving. The smell seemed worse now that his eyes were free.

He swung round. Behind was the entrance they had come in through.

As he had thought: the Door of No Return. A strong

gate of metal bars, set in a hefty stone wall, hundreds of years old. Outside, through the bars, a shining hot day, a blue rolling sea, huge birds wheeling, the beach blinding, hot, hot sunshine. This side, a tiny, horrible, acrid stone room.

And through that door the slaves left, and never saw Africa again.

I have returned through the Door of No Return, he thought.

I am being taken away by people I do not belong to. As my parents were.

He couldn't even struggle and shout again. It was useless, hopeless.

After a while the sailor came over to him. Without looking Charlie in the eye, he removed the gag and hooked the handcuffs to a bar in the wall. There was a piece of sacking cloth nailed up over the gate, rolled back like a blind. He let it down, and went over to the other side of the cell, where he sat with his back to the wall and stared at Charlie through the sudden, almost complete darkness.

Charlie coughed and sucked saliva back into his mouth so he could spit out the dirty taste. Then he closed his eyes and, uncomfortably half hanging from the bar, attempted to achieve something related to a doze, or a trance, or any other way of mentally not being where he was, because where he was was unbearable.

*

Outside the prison, Sergei, salt-encrusted and battered from his marine crossing on board Madame Baleine, curled up in a patch of shade. It was small, but it was all he could find. Yet again, he was waiting for Charlie bliddy Ashanti, in an unlikely place. It was hard work being loyal – why on earth was he doing it? He thought for a bit, and couldn't quite remember. Oh well.

He fell asleep.

Far out in the Atlantic, the two ships bearing Charlie's friends and relations continued to pursue him – in the wrong direction. *Suleiman's Joy* led the way west, with Magdalen and Aneba aboard, followed by *El Baraka*, carrying the Lions, King Boris and Claudio. Their prey, *Old Yeller*, was way behind, way south, waiting.

Not that any of the people aboard any of those ships knew this, of course.

Magdalen and Aneba spent the weeks of the voyage staring out over the endless waves, their stupor broken only by Suleiman's five-times-a-day prayers.

The Young Lion and Elsina were having more fun. Their hiding place in Claudio's cabin had lasted for about half an hour. King Boris spotted them, but, unlike Claudio, he was delighted to see them.

'My dears!' he had shouted. 'How magnificent! Let us pass the time of this wearisome voyage by learning each other's language. Tell me, what do you call this, in Lion?' and he pointed to the porthole.

The Young Lion gave him such a look that Elsina got the giggles.

'We call it strange round thing through which mighty man looks out over the dreadful sea when riding in his sea chariot,' she said. 'What do you call it?'

King Boris was still gazing keenly at them. Of course he had not heard or picked up what she had said, for Cat is spoken as much with the ears and the whiskers as with noises.

'Port, hole,' said King Boris patiently. 'Port. Hole.'

The Young Lion rolled over (as best he could in the small cabin) and put his paws over his face. 'It's going to be a long journey,' he murmured.

Younus, not surprisingly, practically had hysterics when King Boris announced before dinner that there were two Lions aboard who needed feeding too. But hysterical or not, there is very little you can do if you are on a ship with two Lions and two men who want to protect them. Younus's first urge may have been a natural self-protective desire to throw them overboard, but that wasn't going to happen. So he had to be satisfied with trotting nervously around the boat, jumping at every noise, refusing to enter any part without Claudio going in first, and muttering that James Bond never had to deal with Lions.

Elsina and the Young Lion ignored him, mostly. It seemed the kindest thing to do.

Between ignoring Younus, laughing at King Boris and scrapping with each other, they had plenty to do. Only Claudio worried them, because he was looking worried. As well he might – he was in limbo, stuck in the middle of the ocean, with nothing to do but wait and imagine what was waiting for them at the other end of this crossing.

Oh, and on board *Old Yeller*, Rafi sat in his old place in the hold, chained up, surveyed by a bored sailor, and wondered why on earth Charlie had helped him.

Charlie was woken by murmuring voices, and looked up to see four dark eyes, the whites shining in the dimness, staring at him.

'What the –?' he said.

The eyes were scared. Their murmuring rose like alarmed birds and then settled again.

'Who are you?' said Charlie quietly. He said it in Twi. The sailor wouldn't speak Twi – he was Moroccan.

'Seventeen,' came a murmured reply – a low, young, female, African voice.

'Twenty-One,' murmured another – or was it the same one?

Then: 'Who are you?' said the first – or was it the other?

'Charlie,' he said.

One of them laughed. 'Hey, Charlie, we know you are Charlie. But who are you?'

For a moment Charlie smiled too. In Ghana everyone is called Charlie – it's like 'you there' or 'mate' or 'man' or 'you guys'.

'I really am Charlie,' he said. 'It's my name. Who are you?'

'Seventeen,' came the reply.

'Twenty-One,' came the other.

'Hey, I don't need to know how old you are,' Charlie said, though actually they sounded about his own age.

'We really are Seventeen and Twenty-One,' one of them said. 'Those are *our* names.'

'Why?' said Charlie, interested.

'Because when we were born that is how many plaits we each had on our heads,' said one of them.

Charlie was stumped. 'What do you mean?'

'We came out of our mother ready-plaited! We are twins – we did it ourselves inside.'

'What!' cried Charlie.

'It was boring in there!' said the other – Seventeen, Charlie thought it was. He could tell she was smiling. 'Nothing to do, so we plaited.'

Charlie tried to picture two unborn babies happily plaiting each other's hair inside their mother's belly. For a second, a small second, he laughed.

'Shut up!' yelled the sailor suddenly, in Arabic.

They all three turned his way nervously, and shut up.

Much later, Charlie asked quietly, 'Why are you here?'

There was a pause before the sad response. Charlie thought perhaps they had fallen asleep. But then a small voice came out of the darkness: 'We were stolen, we think. Only a few days ago. We live near Kumasi, but we don't know where we are now. Only that we are on the coast.'

Charlie breathed out softly. Stolen. Well, this was turning out to be a regular business.

'Why were you stolen?' he asked, but as he asked, he thought he knew.

'The boys were brought from somewhere else,' Seventeen was continuing.

Charlie looked up.

'What boys?'

'Them,' she said, and he could sense a movement, gesturing behind her. 'They are still sleeping. They have been asleep too long.'

Charlie glanced at the sailor. He was just sitting, his eyes shut. He looked half asleep but ready to wake, relaxed but prepared. He knew Charlie wasn't going anywhere.

Charlie craned to see beyond the dark shapes of the girls. He could make out nothing. No, hang on – was that a doorway?

'Is there another . . . room?' he asked into the darkness.

'Another dungeon,' said the voice of Twenty-One. 'We know what it is here. We have been praying.' There was a trace of tears in her voice. Just a trace. 'There is an altar,' she said. 'From before.'

Charlie was struck dumb for a moment by the idea of the slaves of long ago, packed in, sick and stolen, praying to the ancient spirits for release from this hole, trying to make their forest rites in this dungeon . . .

'We put some buttons there before they came to chain us up,' said Seventeen. 'It's all we had.'

They were all silent. The darkness sat around them.

The sailor sighed deeply and shifted position.

Later, Twenty-One asked, 'Have you been stolen too?'

'Yes,' said Charlie. 'And those boys . . .?'

'We think so. They were just pushed in on top of us . . .'

All of them were still thinking about the past. About long-ago people, long dead now, being stolen and pushed.

'What is going to happen to us?' asked Twenty-One quietly. Her accent reminded Charlie of his grandma. He felt a surge of warmth towards these girls. He didn't know what was going to happen, and he didn't know if two girls and an extra gang of boys were going to make things better or worse . . . but he was beginning to understand that his enemies had no shame.

'I don't know,' he said.

'But I think we are in it together,' said Seventeen.

'Yes,' said Charlie. 'I think we are.'

'Shut up,' said the sailor.

They shut up.

CHAPTER TEN

The first thing Aneba and Magdalen noticed, apart from endless waves, endless sky, and more endless waves, was that one morning there was reception again on their telephones.

'We must be nearing land,' said Magdalen, up on deck, holding her cup of coffee and staring determinedly to the west, as if by staring she could bring the land into view.

'Hey – I've got messages,' said Aneba.

Magdalen immediately flicked round to him.

'It's Mabel,' he said. Then smiled. It was like dawn after a long and restless night.

He passed his phone to Magdalen. 'We were right,' he said. 'There is no official Corporacy Community in the Caribbean, but there is, apparently, listed under the international land ownership regulations, a Corporacy warehouse on the island of San Antonio. It's north-east of Cuba, very small.'

'San Antonio, eh?' said Magdalen. Their spirits lifted for the first time in weeks. 'San Antonio, here we come.'

It turned out to be not such a long way away.

'Beautiful,' said Suleiman as they approached, and indeed it was. Their first view was a wild coastline of cliffs and rocks, high and fierce, with mountains behind and waves crashing at its feet. Heavy greenery festooned the higher clifftops, thick and lustrous, swamped regularly by the salt spray from the crashing Atlantic waves surging in against them. Rainbows sparkled and danced in the flying spume. It was magnificent.

'I will not land here,' said Suleiman.

They continued round to the south side of the island, at a fair distance.

'With cliffs like that you don't really need security,' observed Aneba. 'But there will be a way in, and it will be protected.'

The island's harbour appeared soon enough. It was a smallish cove, on the south-western end of the island. It was immediately recognizable because on the spit of land that protected it from the Atlantic surf, there was a tall metal mast, and from the mast bristled cameras, wires, chip boxes and lord knows what other state-of-the-art security paraphernalia. The cove within looked like paradise – palms, jetties and a shady beach – but the mast was not letting anyone through.

As *Suleiman's Joy* moved west, one of the cameras was following her progress.

'They already know we're here,' said Magdalen.

'Oh, we're not here,' said Aneba. 'We're just passing by, going about our business . . . Best get below – we don't want to be recorded.'

'Tum ti tum ti tum,' hummed Magdalen.

Suddenly Aneba twitched his nostrils. 'Did you get that?' he said.

'What?' said Magdalen.

'That smell.'

Magdalen turned her head in the breeze, trying to catch the scent that had made Aneba jump. And then she did. A sweet, cool scent, very attractive, refreshing, mmm, it made you want to keep breathing it . . .

'Oh!' she cried. 'It's the – it's that sedative thing that they used in Vence. Ugh, I'd recognize it anywhere. Ugh.' She held her nose swiftly, and turned away to the other side of the ship.

'Well, we're definitely in the right place then, aren't we?'

'Sure, but how can we go there? That stuff had both of us stupefied before . . .'

Aneba thought. 'Well,' he said, 'the rose petals I used on you at Vence helped a lot, even though they were weak . . . If we could find a stronger rose – *Canina titularium*, or La Belle Sultane, or the White Queen Elizabeth – and a staple respiratory preventer . . .'

'Suleiman,' said Magdalen. 'Where's the best market round here? Fruit and veg, herbs and spices and flowers?'

Suleiman pored over his charts.

'For eating,' he said, 'Santiago de Cuba. For . . . other purposes . . .' He fell silent.

Aneba looked over Suleiman's shoulder at the chart. 'Ah,' he said.

'What is it?' Magdalen asked. She too peered at the chart. 'Oh,' she said. Then she laughed. 'Well,' she said, 'in a way, it's perfect. I mean . . .'

What they had all seen on the chart was the island of Hispaniola, not so far out of their way. On Hispaniola is the dead land formerly known as Haiti. In Haiti, when it existed as a nation, was Port-au-Prince. In Port-au-Prince was voodoo. And in voodoo circles, you could buy any herb or spice or other peculiar ingredient known – or unknown – to man.

But Haiti was also one of the most godforsaken lands known to man, seemingly cursed since the Europeans slaughtered the two million Indians who had lived on Hispaniola and replaced them with African slaves. Death and poverty and violence had always hung over the island. And now it was manforsaken too, to a large extent, after the floods and earthquakes of the early twenty-first century. Mountains had tumbled, rivers had burst their banks, lakes had joined up and much of the pure water had become salt.

But it remained the home of voodoo, and voodoo was strong and much misunderstood, and in these desperate times survivors turned to it even more.

'Take us there,' said Aneba. 'If the ingredients I need are available anywhere, then it'll be in Port-au-Prince.'

Suleiman muttered a prayer under his breath.

Each time a ship passed close by San Antonio, a camera noticed, and a statutory alert went out from Intelligence and Security, telling those who needed to know. It appeared on their computer screens, or via the internal microchip communications system that was inserted under the skin behind the ear of all Corporacy staff.

The Head Chief Executive had asked to be informed of any unusual shipping, and the alert came up on his screen. He redirected his page to the security camera for that sector, and took a good look at *Suleiman's Joy*. It wasn't identified on his database of international shipping, but that wasn't surprising – Poor World boats often weren't licensed. But he could see it was Poor World, African, sea-battered, too small for the journey it had undertaken.

He froze the image and zoomed in. No one visible on deck matched the descriptions of Charlie, Aneba or Magdalen.

He sent a message to Intelligence and Security: keep an eye on the ship. Get images of those on board. You never know.

CHAPTER ELEVEN

As the night drew on, even Charlie's sailorguard couldn't take the smell in the slave dungeon. He pulled off the sacking that had been hanging over the door. Through the black bars were revealed stars, glowing far away in the hazy hot night sky. There was a little breeze still off the sea, but it didn't reach in to stir the damp, fetid air. Outside was the noise of crickets, an owl's hoot, some music from far away, drumming. And the low, ceaseless roar of the sea.

The girls were sleeping. Their breathing was soft and they seemed remarkably peaceful given that they too were chained to the wall, and had nothing but the bare damp floor to sleep on. Next door was a different matter — odd cries and mutterings had been coming from there all evening.

It was *so* hot.

A tiny voice spoke in Charlie's ear.

'Do you want me to go somewhere?' it whispered. 'I tried to get past the cloth on the door, but it was too heavy for me. I could go now . . . Find Sergei . . . It might be safer at night.'

Ninu! Charlie inclined his head towards him in a friendly fashion. He couldn't stroke him because he was still hung up to the bar (and his shoulders were feeling the pain of it), but he wanted to show his pleasure that Ninu was there.

'I was scared!' said Ninu. 'Nearly got squashed! You and me both!'

'Are you OK?' Charlie whispered.

'Yeah,' said Ninu.

The owl hooted again.

'Don't go out,' said Charlie. Apart from the owl, there were vultures. Charlie had seen them earlier, soaring beautifully like eagles, but with their giveaway tiny bald heads. And the big tricolour lizards – he didn't know what they'd make of Ninu. Anyone might want to eat him. 'Stay here till we've thought something out.'

Thought something out! Well, they couldn't just think themselves out of this fort, that was for sure. More's the pity.

Across the way, the sailor opened one eye. Wearily, he pulled himself up. Ninu scurried behind Charlie's neck, but the sailor just said 'Shut up' again, before letting his eyes droop closed.

Charlie was so scared. Now that he was under constant surveillance, how could he ask Ninu or Sergei to find out for him where they were being taken, or what Maccomo's plan was?

He couldn't.

So did he just have to wait and see?

He stared over at the sailor. What could bring a grown man to keep children prisoners?

Where was his humanity?

Hmm, thought Charlie. Maybe he would look for it. Maybe if he could find the man's humanity, remind him of it, challenge it . . .

But before he got a chance, the next thing happened.

First, a harsh rattling at the gate. Then a crowd of sailors, and with them Majid, squeezing through the dark portal, swarming into the dungeon. Then Maccomo, aloof and authoritative. Then a squawking and a silencing as the boys – there were quite a few of them – and the girls and Charlie were dragged to their feet, unhitched from their hooks and bars, and bustled, still bound, stiff, half asleep, out into the night.

The air, hot as it was, was welcome. It seemed nearly as wet as the sea.

The small boat was right there on the beach. Beyond, in the dull moonlight, Charlie could make out *Old Yeller* waiting for them in the deeper water.

One of the boys was fussing and shouting. A swipe to the head from a sailor shut him up.

'Careful of them!' hissed Maccomo. 'We need them in good shape!'

Charlie swapped quick, nervous glances with Seventeen and Twenty-One. They said nothing.

And then they were in the boat – loads of them, it seemed.

'Sorry,' Charlie muttered automatically as he trod on someone.

'Eh, Charlie,' said a male voice – Ghanaian, between boy and man. 'Worse things happen – like worse things are happening right now.'

For a moment Charlie thought he was being addressed by name – but no, it was the general Ghanaian Charlie.

And then, in the moonlight, he looked at the boy he had stepped on – and he squawked aloud. 'Jake Yeboa!' he said, and then shut himself up. The boy shot him a look.

Jake Yeboa! Number ten for the Starlets!

'It is you, isn't it?' Charlie whispered.

'Yes,' replied the boy. 'It's all of us! Who are you?'

But Charlie wasn't interested in answering. He knew who he was. What he wanted to know was what in heck Maccomo was doing stealing the entire Ghanaian junior national football team.

And then suddenly he did know. He knew exactly.

Being able to talk Cat? Braiding before you are born? Discovering a cure for asthma? Being simply the best junior football team the world has ever seen?

This had Corporacy written all over it. They were after the talent again.

*

Suleiman's Joy glided past the Isle of Gonaïve into Port-au-Prince on heavy glutinous seas, under a hot sky. Mists were rolling over the mountainous interior of Hispaniola, and a sweaty, unrefreshing rain hung about in the air.

Aneba shook his head as he looked ashore. A tatty concrete quay ran out into the harbour, sprouting shafts of twisted metal, and some low, weather-stained buildings lay along the seafront. A ragged flag slumped on a rusty flagpole. There was nobody around.

'Well, we don't have to stay too long,' he murmured. Then he turned to Suleiman.

'Give me two hours,' he said. 'Wait offshore. Then return every hour on the hour, and I'll signal to you.'

Magdalen bit the inside of her cheek. Of course it made more sense for Aneba to go, and to go without her – there might be Corporacy spies here who would report on the big black man and the red-haired woman – but she didn't want to let him go. She pressed her fingernails into her palms.

'Bye,' he said shortly.

'Bye,' she said.

The main market was right there by the harbour. It seemed merchants didn't want to hang around too long here, or go too far inland. Aneba picked his way across what had once been a road, avoiding the deepest potholes, but even so his shoes caked up with sloppy mud. He glanced over the stalls:

vegetables, batteries, guns, chemicals. One was offering hormones, vitamins and viruses. Another had scraggy chickens. He glanced around him. The stallholders were skinny and blank-faced. Business was not booming. He didn't want to look too obviously a stranger, but equally he needed someone to tell him where to go for what he wanted.

Above the sick smell of the mud came another smell, a fabulous mixed-up aroma of nutmeg and cardamom, black sugar and ginger, tea tree and rose. Spices. Aneba followed the smell. He knew exactly what he wanted. He'd identified it when they'd been imprisoned at Vence, and he knew he'd find it here, but he wasn't seeing it.

He stopped for a coffee at a stand with a tattered cloth roof.

'*Tu cherches quelque chose de spécial?*' asked a soft voice beside his elbow. Are you looking for something special? '*De l'opium? Du hashish? Du peyote?*'

Aneba looked round. He didn't want opium, hashish or peyote, but someone who could supply those things might also have what he needed.

'*J'ai besoin de quelque chose, oui,*' he replied.

A child was standing there, barefoot, half invisible in the shadows.

'*Viens,*' she said, and scooted across the lane, down an alley. The buildings were half ruined – rooms falling off them, wires sticking out of them, mud seeping, seeping everywhere under the fine rain. She slipped into a dark doorway beneath a shabby ornamental balcony. Aneba followed after her, his feet heavy with claggy mud. The building was painted pale green, and the paint was peeling off.

'*Attends*,' she said, and his eyes started to get used to the dimness.

He could hear voices inside, talking a kind of French, only it wasn't French.

'*Kisa saa-a ye?*' said an old voice, male, dusty.

'*Gin oun gason, boko*,' said the child. '*Apa.*'

'*Moun ki peyi li ye?*'

Aneba couldn't understand. He waited. There was a dead mouse half buried in the mud of the floor, and the sole of an old shoe. He wondered if the house had been built on a rubbish dump.

Soon the child returned. Following her was an old man.

Aneba knew all too well that there would follow a long preamble, a lot of talk and courtesy, waiting, making of excuses, arguing about prices . . . Everything in him wanted to yell, 'Cut to the chase! Let's get down to business!' But he knew it had to take the time it had to take.

In the end it was only an hour and a half, including discussing the exact recipe (the old man was very knowledge-able) and locating the additional ingredients. Aneba came back up the alley carrying two large and one small sealed bottles of maximum-strength essence of exactly what he wanted, plus the information that, although it was hard to find processed, the rose that was the main ingredient grew wild in various places around the islands, if you knew where to look.

He had checked the essence. It was the real thing. He sat on the concrete quay and waited.

When *Suleiman's Joy* appeared, he felt a ripple of relief.

But as the boat approached, he stood up. There was a figure on deck – a man. He didn't look like Suleiman, or either of the sailors. He was more slender – fairer. Magdalen was on deck too, talking to the new man. Chatting. Happily. She turned and waved to Aneba.

He was still wary as he stepped aboard.

'Mag?' he said questioningly.

Her face was full of a big grin.

'Did you get it?' she asked.

'Yes,' he said. 'Plenty. But, er –' He gestured to the blond man – and as he did so, he recognized him. It was Charlie's Venetian friend.

Aneba couldn't help himself. He flung his arms round Claudio and gave him an immense bear hug.

'You came!' he said. 'You really came! Did you follow us all the way here? My god – you must be Charlie's real friend. Wow. Wow,' and he hugged him again.

Suleiman hadn't even moored the boat. He was taking off again without any hesitation, muttering his prayers.

'And it's not just Claudio!' cried Magdalen. 'He's brought –'

'Who?' Aneba smiled.

'Well. Any person who is not crazy would maybe not believe it,' began Claudio.

'Try me,' suggested Aneba.

'The King of Bulgaria and two Lions,' said Claudio. Aneba was silenced. He stared.

'Um – also Charlie's loyal friends?' he said finally.

'Yes,' said Claudio. 'Yes, they came for Charlie.'

'Oh, my word,' said Aneba. 'Where are they?'

'On board our boat. Is called *El Baraka*. We just arrive in this dreadful place, following you, and we see this your boat, so I board – we are offshore. You can come and see. Please.' He gestured out to sea. In the distance, Aneba could make out another small ship.

'Glad to,' he said. 'Glad to.'

Once his cargo was safely aboard *Old Yeller*, Maccomo made his telephone call to the Chief Executive.

The Chief Executive wanted him to bring the merchandise to him in Vence. Maccomo refused.

'I go straight to the top,' he said. 'There has been too much nonsense. I will not risk my investment.'

So the CE rang the HCE, and the HCE smiled happily because he had been right. Charlie was coming to him, and where Charlie came, his parents could not be too far behind. He'd just carry on keeping his eyes open.

*

The crossing, for Charlie, was just dull and unpleasant –
or rather it was curiously suspended, because he knew it
was going to get scary, but it wasn't actually scary yet. He
wasn't too seasick, though he would have given a great deal
for some fresh air and clear sunshine. But, incarcerated, he
soon forgot that outside the walls of his wooden cell was
the vast Atlantic Ocean, filling the basin of the world,
stretching for thousands of miles, deep and wide. Under
other circumstances what an adventure it would have been,
to cross the Atlantic by boat! But it was not. He was in a
tiny, stuffy cabin with no company but for his beady-eyed
sailorguard and Ninu, who dared not even show his little
green face.

Charlie didn't know where any of the others were – not
Rafi, not Seventeen and Twenty-One, and not the Starlets.
He imagined that they might be all together somewhere,
without him. Part of him was a tiny bit flattered to be put
on his own. He knew why Maccomo had done it: Maccomo
now knew that Charlie was clever. Charlie could no longer
kid him that he was dim and docile. Maccomo had put him
on his own expressly *because* he didn't trust him not to come
up with another plan for escape.

And, of course, he did entirely intend to come up with
some such plan.

But what? How?

He tried his hardest, sitting in that dim cupboard, to
keep hold of his bravery, his brains, his good sense – all the

things that had helped him so far. But it was harder than ever before. He had lost his parents, again. The stakes were higher, he was more alone, and more powerless. No daylight, no fresh air. A bowl or two of not very nice slop each day.

And there was another sorrow. He didn't know if Sergei was on board. He couldn't send Ninu to find out; they could hardly even talk. Charlie was watched all the time and Ninu was still in his pocket, coming out only during the brief moments when the sailor snoozed, to catch mosquitoes and boat bugs with his long, extraordinary tongue.

Charlie sat on the rough wooden floor, carefully so as not to squash Ninu, and stroked the back of his frilled head. Apart from that contact, Charlie was alone, all the way across the Atlantic, for thousands of long and lonely sea miles.

He couldn't even liven his time by wondering where they were going. He knew. They were going to some bigwig Corporacy place. Some Gated Community mastermind mothership central office headquarters. Some dreadful place, where the doctored air his parents had told him about would befuddle his mind, and he would be lost to himself and the world, powerless. No one was going to kill him or beat him or hurt him. They were just going to soak him up until he didn't exist any more. His body would putter blindly about, but his self, his Charlieness, would be gone. He could not think of any way round it. And he tried. Lord, he tried. In that dim little room, he drove himself round in dismal circles with the idea that he must be able to do something, to think of something, to prevent this from happening. But he could think of nothing. Sometimes he thought of how ashamed he was to be thinking of nothing, but mostly he just thought of nothing.

CHAPTER
TWELVE

Charlie had been sitting in his despondency for some weeks when a charming young woman with shiny hair and a freckly nose knocked on the door, beamed at the sailor and invited Charlie to come and join her on deck.

'Hi!' she said. 'I'm Sally-Ann, welcome! I'm your Assigned Companion! We've been expecting ya! I guess where you've been sleeping hasn't been too comfortable — but never mind, you're here now!'

The sunlight blinded him as he came out on to the deck. Blue, blue sky. Brightness everywhere. The sea sparkled up at him, and a tiny bright bird buzzed past. It's heaven, he thought confusedly. This is the beginning of the end. His breath caught in his throat. I'm going to start breathing that stuff Mum and Dad told me about and this is the last thought I will have that will be mine . . . He coughed. He could smell the sweetness on the air.

'Where am I?' Charlie said as Sally-Ann led him on to a pretty wooden jetty. He knew, but he wanted to know the name. He wanted to be intelligent and logical while he still could. And where were Seventeen and Twenty-One? And the Starlets? And Rafi?

'San Antonio!' she said with a little laugh, stepping down on to a beach that could only accurately be described as perfect – the palest of pink sand, bluest of turquoise seas, lightest of halcyon breezes, gentlest of caressing suns. The contrast with the dim cabin in which he had crossed the ocean, or with his dim mood, could not have been greater.

'And where's that?' he asked, smiling back at her.

'Why, it's here, of course!' she said.

She led him across the beach on to a track, where a little electric tram waited for them. For about ten minutes it carried them silently through a natural paradise of rocks and beach, sandy dunes and graceful trees. Little monkeys chattered in the branches, and more tiny hummingbirds spun between flowers four times their size, glittering in the sunlight like scattered jewels from a broken necklace. And the air was sweet. Charlie put his fingers to his mouth and nose, tried to feel the inside of his lungs. Was it in him yet? Was it affecting him?

Soon enough the tram drew up to a smooth green lawn, where they got off. Sally-Ann led Charlie towards a rather glamorous hut. It was made of strong wooden poles, and its walls were mostly billowy gauzy curtains. The floor was marble. It seemed to be a bedroom. A gaggle of bright parrots sat in a row on the roofbeam, then with a tremendous racket took off, flashing their brilliant underwings.

'Look!' Sally-Ann said, pointing round the corner of the veranda that surrounded the hut. There was a huge shower, there in the open air, sheltered from public gaze (not that there seemed to be any public) by a floaty tumble of purply-pink flowers. But as Charlie looked closer, he saw that it wasn't actually a shower. It was a fountain. Warm. For washing in.

'I'll bring you some clean things,' she said nicely.

Charlie smiled blankly. The beauty, the kindness, the fresh air, the sunshine – it was too much for him. As Sally-Ann turned away, Charlie gently put Ninu and his medicine and his mother's Improve-Everything Lotion in a pile on the enormous bed. Ninu and he looked at each other.

'There are probably hidden cameras everywhere,' Charlie murmured in Cat.

Ninu narrowed his eyes and valiantly did his best to look like a plastic toy.

In the fountain, the weeks of salt and sweat and dirt washed off Charlie in great slooshes of refreshing, palm-shaded coolness. That part was plainly wonderful. He grabbed the soap and scrubbed at his nappy head, frothed up his armpits and even washed between his toes. The fountain of water jetted up out of the ground. The delicious scent of the air was so easy to breathe . . . Perhaps, he thought, if I stand under the water, less air will get into me . . .

That's a stupid thing to think.

San Antonio

The lift

— Where the Sweet Air comes from

The huge shower

The glamorous huts

Junior Education Unit

Psychological Benevolence Unit

The perfect beach

Landing jetty

Electric tram track

SCALE: from here to here = NO DISTANCE AT ALL

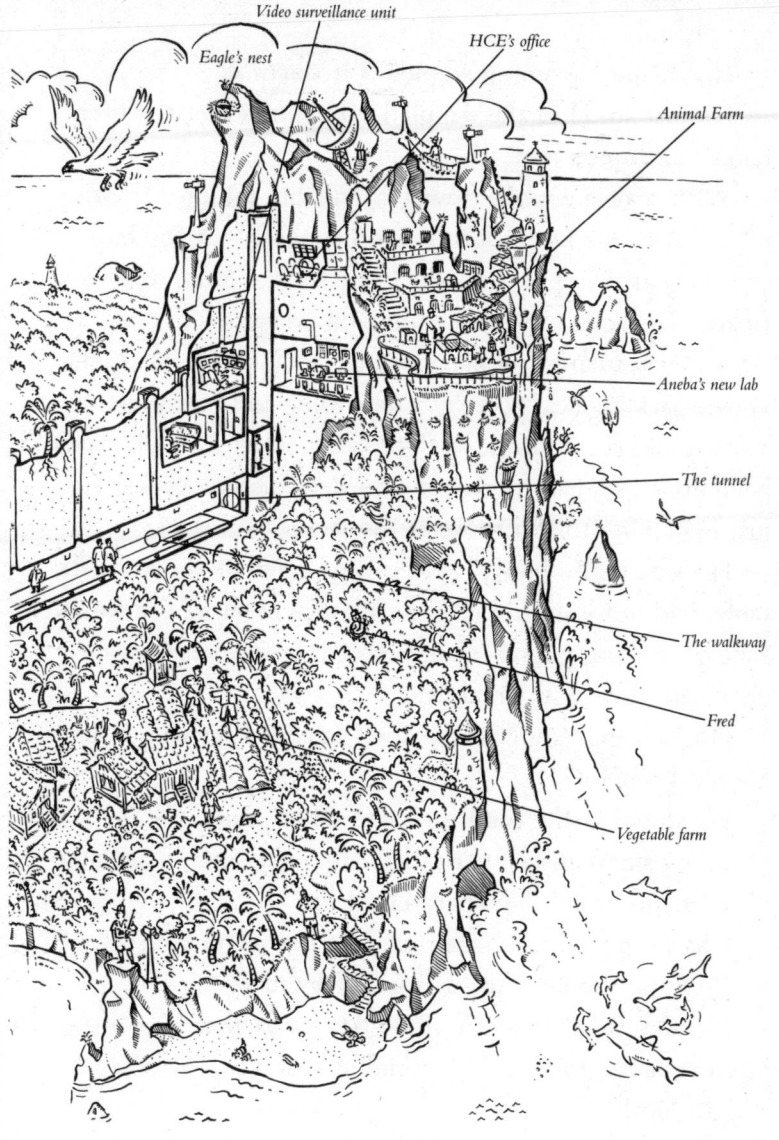

Eagle's nest

Video surveillance unit

HCE's office

Animal Farm

Aneba's new lab

The tunnel

The walkway

Fred

Vegetable farm

Is that me becoming stupid? Is it starting?

He just stood in the dappled sunlight and let the fountain's fall drench him.

With a clean white towel round his middle, Charlie returned to his hut. Clothes had been laid out for him – cool easy trousers and a T-shirt. He looked around for his jacket – there it was, safely hung on a chair.

As he returned to the veranda, he looked out at the view: sparkling sea, rustling palms toing and froing gently, a sweep of green hillside so fluffy and perfect, it could have been done by a hairdresser, and beyond, the fine yellow sun just beginning to slip towards the west.

He was really hungry. He caught sight of the veranda table, laid out with – well, a really nice meal. There was a slice of salmon, potato salad, beans, mayonnaise, mangoes, chocolate cake with cream.

Do they put stuff in the food as well? he wondered. Should I not eat?

He stared at the food for quite a long time.

I can't starve myself to death, he thought. There's nothing else for me to eat. Nowhere else I can go.

Charlie pulled up a chair and started to tuck in.

Well, he thought, this is really very nice.

He was shocked at the thought – was that him being brainwashed? How could he think it was nice – it was getting to him!

He put down his fork and went inside.

One of the veils had been drawn back to reveal a television. Charlie hadn't watched telly since he didn't know when. And he'd never watched a telly like this – its plasma screen was the size of half the wall.

He stretched out on the bed with the remote control and began to channel-surf. Comedies, films, football games, family fun, quizzes, more comedies, baseball games, snooker, news, more films, murder programmes, detective programmes, pop music, ads, ads, ads . . .

Were the ads getting inside his head? Were there subliminal messages in among the programmes, affecting his brain?

He watched for hours.

He fell asleep.

In the video surveillance unit, Sally-Ann turned to Seventeen's Assigned Companion, who was watching Seventeen doing exactly the same thing in a hut across the way from Charlie's, and said cheerfully, 'Excellent! Charlie seems to be settling right in! How's your girl doing?'

'Doing just fine!' said the other companion with a friendly smile. 'I think they're all going to be really happy with us!'

And in the HCE office, the HCE, listening through his commchip, smiled too.

*

From his hiding place in *Old Yeller*'s one tatty lifeboat, Sergei had watched Charlie go ashore. He'd rested his chin on his paws, and thought, I hope he's as tough as his old parents. I hope he's tougher.

And then he'd brought his back legs up to perch on the bulwark of the boat between his forelegs, before shooting himself swiftly on to the jetty. Under the shrubbery for purposes of discretion, he'd followed Charlie and the young woman to the tram, then hopped up on to the back as they settled in the front.

After Sally-Ann had left the hut, Sergei tried to gain Charlie's attention while he was showering, but the fountain made quite a racket and Sergei was extremely reluctant to get closer because he did not like getting wet. (Riding the whale had been different — a matter of life and death.) He considered approaching Charlie while he was eating, but Charlie was deeply engrossed, and the table was exposed. Until he knew more about what was going on Sergei was reluctant to make himself visible. Ditto when Charlie was watching telly — Sergei made look-at-me faces outside until he had cheekache, but Charlie was staring at the screen, and nothing would shift his gaze.

'You can see him goin' square-eyed,' muttered Sergei in disgust. He resolved to try after dark. The surveillance systems would be less effective. He wasn't going to get spotted and carted off for god knows what by these weirdo humans, thank you very much.

CHAPTER
THIRTEEN

Maccomo, having handed over his charges to their Sally-Anns, had been guided by his Assigned Guest Coordinator, a plump boy called Dave, to the HQ of the HQ. This was a comfortable chamber with low couches, marble floors, air conditioning and a wall of telly screens on which the occupants could watch anything that was going on, anywhere on the island.

He was welcomed by the Head Chief Executive. 'Maccomo!' he cried happily, as though they were old friends, though, in fact, they hadn't ever met before. 'Good to see ya, good to see ya. See ya've brought the full cargo along! All ticked off! Good to see those two little girls – quick fingers is an area we've been a little delayed in, to tell the truth, so new input there is good noos, the market is crying out for quick fingers, so we can get straight in to work on that. And the football team – well, wow! All a' them! But, of course, the prize of the lot – Maccomo, you pulled it off! The Catspeaker! What can I say? You prarbly know we had a little trouble over in Yurp with the parents

. . . But thanks to you that's all over. They'll be here lickety-split, I'll bet, and we'll have all the ingredients we need for a fine and profitable noo season a'research.'

Maccomo smiled quietly. How right he was about humanity, to expect nothing of them. How very low they all were. Money or sentimentality, that was what counted for human beings.

'Ya've earned ya fee, sir, yes indeed,' the Head Chief Executive continued, 'and I truly hope that you'll be working with us again in the near future, because frankly, we cain't always find contractors a' your calibre. We've had some failures in the field who have not been efficient in their collection agencies.'

'I know,' said Maccomo. He was uncomfortable here and wanted to move on. The air smelt funny. It turned his stomach, and for the first time in a while he thought of the Lionmedicine he used to take. 'I know – I have brought him too. Rafi Sadler.'

'Have ya now!' cried the Head Chief Executive, who, of course, knew perfectly well that he had (Intelligence and Security had told him). 'Ain't that good noos! You're bringin' me nothin' but good noos! He can join the programme along of all the other folks, and I dare say he'll be far the better man for it.'

This kind of phrase meant nothing to Maccomo. Some optimistic Empire catchphrase. It bored him and he was ready to leave.

'I will take the fee you would have paid him, in payment, plus my own fee,' said Maccomo. 'Now I go.'

'Where you off to so quick?' enquired the Head Chief Executive. 'Maybe you could stick around – we'll be needing ya again, sure as eggs is eggs!'

Maccomo did not interest himself in eggs.

'My ship is returning to Africa,' he said civilly but coldly. 'I have business to attend to. So . . .'

'Course! Of course!' said the HCE. 'We'll get your fee and all for ya by tomorrow. Spend a night or two, have some rest, and the Marine Resources Maintenance Unit can give your ship a look-over after your journey.' With a cheerful thumbs-up sign, he ushered Maccomo out into the care of Dave, who led him to one of the guest houses. The HCE watched on one of his monitors. 'He'll be just fine,' he murmured to himself. 'Just fine.'

Rafi did not, however, join the programme along with the others. He was put instead in the workcamp, which was where the Corporacy kept those people they had kidnapped who turned out to be of no particular use to them. Rafi was given a dormitory bunk next to the World Champion Boiled Egg Eater, whose farts filled the rough-hewn dorm every night, and the former Mr Universe of Smoking, whose wheezing coughs and terrible snoring destroyed any remnant chance of sleep.

During the day they dug the fields and the vegetable

patches. During the night they tossed and turned and coughed and farted.

I might as well've been drowned in that snikin' ship, Rafi thought – his last thought before the Sweet Air got to him. 'If Troy were here, I'd just sleep outside with him.' But he was afraid to sleep outside on his own, with the hooting owls and the creaking insects and the mysterious scrabbling sounds of the Caribbean night, and Troy was not there – he was living happily in the home of a Spanish customs officer who had taken pity on him in the dog pound. Happily, that is, except that he missed Rafi.

On board *El Baraka*, Aneba and Magdalen did their very best not to be amazed by and terrified of Charlie's friends. It wasn't King Boris – he was just a king, they could handle that. But the Lions were something else. They lay calmly in the cabin, twitching their whiskers a little and – the young female in particular – seeming to smile. Charlie's parents were astounded.

'I think they understand a lot when we speak,' said Claudio.

'Hello,' said Magdalen softly. She kind of wanted to hold her hand out, but it seemed crazy. Claudio had filled her in on how they came to be here. These wild cats had willingly, of their own accord, got on to a ship and crossed the Atlantic – stowed away! – for the sake of her son, her boy. She could hardly speak. There were tears in her eyes.

Elsina flicked her tail this way and that.

'I wish I could speak to you like my son does,' said Magdalen. 'I wish I could tell you how amazed I am, how touched I am, that you are here. I wish . . .' But she couldn't.

'Poor thing,' murmured Elsina. 'She looks a bit like Charlie, doesn't she? She must be so worried.'

'If they can understand,' said Aneba, 'they'd better be here for our discussions.'

'Yeah, here's my idea,' said the Young Lion. 'Let's just go and scare some humans and get this over with.' But, of course, no one understood – except Elsina, who rolled her eyes.

'Well, then,' said King Boris to Aneba and Magdalen. 'Tell us what you know.'

They explained their theory about San Antonio and the Corporacy. King Boris, who had already been in touch with Edward, was able to confirm it.

'And are we sure that Charlie is there?' said King Boris.

'No,' said Aneba. 'Which is why I am going to go and find out.'

'How?' they all asked – and Aneba explained his plan.

'I must try to get a job on San Antonio,' he said. 'Look at me.'

He had not shaved for a long time. His hair was rough from the sea air, and long (for him) because it had been a month since they had been in Morocco, when he'd last seen a barber. He was wearing sun-faded trousers and a T-shirt like any T-shirt. 'In the market,' he said, 'I could pass for a local. If I make my eyes dead. I'll go there again tonight, and sniff around, and see what the local talk is about San Antonio.'

Everyone was silent. Nobody wanted him to have to go back there. Everyone knew it was a good idea, though.

'Does he remind you of anyone?' the Young Lion asked Elsina. 'With his plans and his braveness?'

'Yeah, Aneba's just like Charlie,' Elsina said affectionately.

'Yes — but the big difference is, Charlie listens to us,' said the Young Lion. 'With these people it's almost like being back in the Circus. Humans in charge, business as usual.'

The business of the Circus was not, however, going as usual. Tib's Gallimaufry, on board the *Circe*, was crossing the Atlantic well to the north of the other ships. They were heading for New England, where the Show was booked in at towns down the coast for the rest of the summer. Major Tib, however, had received a message.

He was sitting, as so often, in his beautifully carved and panelled cabin, in his long robe, with his feet up on the table and a glass of brandy at his elbow.

'Pirouette!' he yelled.

It was a moment or two before the yell reached her (third-hand via Hans and Sigi Lucidi), and a moment or two more before she could get down from the rigging, where she had been practising balancing.

'Darn promoter's gone bust!' Major Tib yelled when she finally arrived in his doorway. 'Here's me and the best darn Circus either side of any ocean halfway across the darn Atlantic and there's no darn Empire tour! Whaddawe gonna do?'

Pirouette said nothing – she didn't need to. He just wanted an audience. That was why she was there. He was a Ringmaster, after all.

'Well, no darn New England tour . . . heck! Let's go south instead. Carolina's nice . . . Florida? Where's our best contacts, Pirouette?'

She smiled and leaned against a door jamb.

'I'll get on to Milam Dowdy. He'll know what's doing. Dangblammit, what an embarrassment! Or should we head back to Europe?'

She shrugged.

Major Tib got on the phone. 'Dangblammit,' he was mumbling still. But within an hour he had an offer of a tour up the Mississippi, starting from New Orleans.

'New Orleans!' he cried. 'How's about that, Pirouette? Let's turn the ship south and catch a load more fish for them tigers. We're going to New Orleans – gonna see the voodoo king.' He broke into song. Major Tib loved New Orleans. The heat and the gumbo, the ghost stories and the Cajun music. 'I'll treat you all at Tipitina's!' he yelled. 'Brush up ya dancing shoes!'

Major Tib's New Orleans Dancing Blues

R. LOCKHART

Pirouette shook her head, and went to tell the captain that Major Tib wanted to see him.

That evening Aneba went ashore again, and after a night over which we will draw a veil (spent mainly in muddy-floored shacks that served as low drinking dives), he came back in the radiant toxic-pink Caribbean dawn tired and depressed but with useful information.

'Nobody goes there,' he said. 'Nobody can get ashore. The people here hate San Antonio. It has everything they haven't: law and order, money, comfort. But at the same time, they say, it's a sick place, a place without soul. They say people's eyes are dead who live there, that their smiles are painted on. One said, "At least we *know* we live in hell." And anyway – yes – all the staff are hired by the international personnel department, all references are checked, there are no vacancies and even if there were, they would not hire locally.'

'Oh,' said Magdalen.

'There is only one possibility,' continued Aneba.

Magdalen looked at him expectantly.

'There is a woman who comes to market – to the spices and potions market. No one could tell me what she buys there. Her name is Auntie Auntie. They say she's powerful on San Antonio, and that she is African. They assume she is a witch, coming for ingredients. She comes most weeks. She is expected the day after tomorrow.'

'So, will you seduce her? Make her fall in love with you? Or kidnap her? Save her life?'

'Save her life, I think. Africans care about things like that. Even powerful ones working for the Corporacy.'

'So . . .'

'So I think you will have to try to kill her – unless I can get someone else to. Simplest to keep it in the family.'

Magdalen sighed. 'It's risky,' she said. 'She may have security.'

'You'll have to hire a car, I suppose, and knock her down. I could show up her guards – beat them at something.'

'Be serious,' said Magdalen.

'I am being,' Aneba said. 'Unless we can think of something better. Let's sleep on it.'

'I've been asleep all night,' Magdalen said.

'I haven't,' Aneba replied, rolling into his bunk. 'You go and tell the others.'

Magdalen smiled. At least there were others. It was nice to have others to tell.

CHAPTER
FOURTEEN

harlie woke in the morning full of fear.

Was he himself? He did a quick scan of his mind – pictured his mother's face, counted to twenty in Arabic and Italian, remembered his bedroom at home, the tune Claudio sang on his gondola, the embroidery on Major Tib's best Ringmaster tailcoat. All present and correct.

He kicked back the clean white sheet that covered him and did some back bends and a handstand. He ran through his problems – lost parents, prisoner of Corporacy, potential brainwashing by drugged air, Sergei unaccounted for, Maccomo lurking, Rafi . . .

This would be enough to make anyone miserable, but Charlie smiled.

He remembered it all! He knew what was going on, he knew where he was, he knew why. His mind was still his!

How come?

And would it last?

He smiled again. Never mind – he had what he had, and

he would use it while he could. If his mind went later on, too bad, it was all over. He'd worry about that when it happened. For now, he'd survived a night in this air and he felt like a bright boy who'd slept comfortably and eaten well and had a lot to do.

First things first: know your enemy. He knew the Corporacy had created their Gated Communities all over the world to keep rich scared people safe from normal people, and to prevent their employees from ever leaving or wanting to leave. He knew they'd kidnapped his parents. He knew they filled their Gated Communities with this scented chemical that sapped people's initiative and individuality. He knew they had created the Allergenies, genetically modified cats that would make children ill with asthma, so that the Corporacy could keep making lots of money from selling lots of asthma medicine. He knew that Maccomo had brought him here for the same reasons Rafi had tried to – so that the Corporacy could use his skills, or possibly *prevent* him from using them.

But the Corporacy didn't know Charlie. Oh, they'd done their homework – they knew he was a Catspeaker, knew who his parents were, had seen his exam results and knew what foods he liked. But they didn't know him. So he was going to do his trick: he was going to let them think he was doing everything they wanted. Maccomo might be wise to that trick of his, but these people weren't. (And if Maccomo had told them? Well, in his experience people often believed what they wanted to believe. Particularly if it matched what they saw with their own eyes.) And he was going to fight them every inch of the way, invisibly, for as long as he could.

Ninu, who had rather bravely taken up residence on the terrace, and blended in perfectly, looked up and smiled at him as he came outside.

'Hey!' he said to Charlie in Cat. 'Look who's here!'

Why's he speaking Cat? Charlie thought, in the split second before turning to see, sitting under a swathe of dark pink bougainvillea flowers, with a dry expression on his face, none other than Sergei.

'Mornin',' said the scraggy cat.

Charlie was about to fall to his knees and hug Sergei, but he remembered himself just in time. Give nothing away to whoever might be watching!

'Mornin',' he replied, with a little smile tugging at his lips.

'Feeling yourself today, are yer?' enquired Sergei.

Charlie surveyed the twinkling sea below him, and took a full deep breath.

'Feeling great today,' he said, not looking at Sergei. 'Bit annoyed at being kidnapped and locked up, glad this prison is more comfortable than the one on the boat . . .'

'Not, erm, feeling at all, erm, fuzzy-headed? At all?'

'Feeling myself,' said Charlie firmly. 'Full of beans, and about to start finding out what's going on here. Delighted

to be at the root of it all. Ready to go out exploring.'

'Well, well, well,' said Sergei, pleased. 'Look at yer. It had yer mum and dad poleaxed. Yer a tough little candidate, aren't yer?'

'So are you, then,' said Charlie. And in that moment he realized it. 'Hey!' he said.

'What?' enquired Sergei.

'It doesn't affect you, does it?'

'Nope.'

'So – do you think my cat blood is protecting me from it?'

Sergei grinned a slow, crooked, cat grin. 'I would be delighted,' he said, 'if that were the case.'

Magdalen shook Aneba awake.

'Aneba!' she said.

'What?' he replied, cross at being woken.

'They may perfectly well recognize you. They may know that we're coming. If Charlie *is* there, they'll expect us to be following, and to try to rescue him. They'll have their security on us, they may have tracked us from Essaouira. It's too risky!'

Aneba rubbed his eyes. She was right.

'So,' he said.

'So turn it to our advantage.'

'Turn it to our advantage?' he said.

'Make a deal,' she said.

He thought. As he thought, it started to make sense.
He smiled.

'Now,' said Sally-Ann after breakfast, 'your Introduction-
to-the-Corporacy Session!'

It started with a film, run on his screen, that told him
all about how the Corporacy had, since the nineteenth century, been making food and medicine for the people of the
world, making more and better things to make people happier, serving the public and employing people . . . Charlie
listened politely and said, 'How interesting,' every now and
again. Sally-Ann smiled at him. She'd heard about this boy's
parents, and she'd expected that he would be difficult too,
and not understand that all the Corporacy wanted was for
everyone to be happy. But he wasn't difficult — he was
friendly and calm and interested. It would make her job
much easier. She gave him a thumbs-up and ruffled his hair.
Charlie grinned back.

Great, she's falling for it, he thought. I wonder how
much more of this rubbish I'm going to have to listen to.
He knew perfectly well that the Corporacy was a business,
and its main purpose was to make money. That wasn't a
crime, of course — but he knew what it would do to make
money. He wasn't falling for this Corporacy hooey.

Then it was on to the Junior Education Unit. Charlie
checked out the surroundings as Sally-Ann walked him there
— tropical forest to the north and east, with mountains

beyond; sea to the south; flat land to the west. The biggest mountain looked like a volcano – a tall cone. This island was really beautiful. The paths were pale gravel, lined with low lighting; there were many of the pretty huts, and beyond them, inland, some larger, more sturdy buildings, pale, concrete. One of these was the Junior Education Unit, and going into it were Twenty-One and Seventeen.

Charlie hadn't even seen them since they were all in the slave castle together, and he called out to them happily.

'Hey, girls!' he called.

They turned and smiled at him – and as they did, he knew that the Sweet Air was getting to them. Their smiles were large, but they were the smiles of dollies, of empty souls.

'Hello, Charlie!' said Twenty-One, and her voice had something of the tone of Sally-Ann's, like a computer voice. Not the lustrous, intelligent African voice of that night in the dungeon.

'Hello, Charlie!' said Seventeen.

Charlie bit his lip. He wasn't surprised – of course the Sweet Air would get to them. He was just – well, even more aware of what a massive task he had in front of him. It wasn't just he who had to escape this place – it was Seventeen and Twenty-One too. And the Starlets. And maybe others, already here. Only Charlie, of all the people here, had a clear mind. So that gave him a responsibility.

Even if (if!) he could somehow escape, he had to take the others with him.

Where were the Lions when you needed them? Six loyal Lions would be really useful in a situation like this. He smiled at the thought of them. They weren't the most practical of friends to travel around with, but he missed them a lot. Especially the Young Lion.

All he had now was his own brain.

OK, he said to himself. Find out all you can. One step at a time.

Sally-Ann ushered him inside the Junior Education Unit. The Starlets were already there, eighteen of them, sitting in rows. They were all to take some straight academic tests, like at school. Charlie sat down and, between sums (several of which he got wrong on purpose), he glanced about at the footballers. He didn't know them, so it was hard to judge, but they seemed – well, calm and cheerful. Not how a bunch of kidnapped kids should look. Jake Yeboa was sitting behind him, so he couldn't get a good look at him, but he could see Jake's brother Pierre over in the corner. Who wasn't there? Rafi. Well, fair enough – he wasn't one of the special talents. But where was he then? Safely incarcerated by the Corporacy? Or fomenting trouble, a loose cannon that might go off at any time?

Thinking about him, Charlie felt a little prickle of doubt in his belly. What was that line from the *Jungle Book*? We are of one blood, you and I . . .

He didn't want to think about it.

Back to maths: $6x - 2 + 2x = -2 + 4x + 8 \ldots$

That afternoon they were all moved on to the Psychological Benevolence Unit, where smiling helpers tested their personalities with questions and tricks. Charlie found this merely amusing, because he had done some of these with Brother Jerome back in London, with a view to learning how to confuse them. He knew no sensible person would ever use one of these tests, so he enjoyed sabotaging them.

Charlie looked at the paper in front of him.

When walking into a room of people, you:
1. Walk tall and proud, looking everyone in the eye
2. Stoop or hunch your shoulders and avoid looking at anyone
3. Make a loud joke or comment to attract attention
4. Try to be as invisible as possible

The only correct answer (5. It depends on my mood, on who the people are, on whether I know them, on whether they are kids or adults, on whether I'm alone or with my friends or my parents, whether it's a party, or an office, or a shop, or a hospital ward, or someone's bedroom, on whether I'm hungry or tired, whether the people are looking at me or not, making jokes or not, talking or not, smiling or not . . .) wasn't on the list. Charlie ticked 4. (How stupid! Whether you're visible or not depends as much on who's looking at you as on what you yourself are doing.)

The rest of the questions were just as small-minded. Charlie thought carefully before ticking the answers that would make him seem dull and dim and without any personality at all.

At various stages during the day individual kids were ushered out of their tests, one at a time, with a big smile and a friendly hand under the elbow. They didn't come back.

None of the others looked up or around to see who was going, or where. None of them seemed to notice that their friends weren't reappearing. Charlie noticed, though, and wondered.

When he'd finished his personality tests, it was his turn. Sally-Ann with her smile escorted him across the sweeping lawn, further in towards the lush forest. Charlie clocked everything: the thick creepers swirling up to the heights of the canopy, the tall trees with their high snake-tangly roots, the way that Sally-Ann held her palm up to gain entrance to – wow! – a concealed door in the wall of rock.

'That's clever,' he said, making his voice sound younger than it naturally would. 'How do you do that?'

Sally-Ann pointed to a small lump in her palm – the size and shape of a baked bean. 'My identity,' she smiled. 'It's all in there!'

How interesting, thought Charlie. Computerized recognition system of some kind.

The rock slid open for her.

'Come along!' she sang, and Charlie followed her.

Inside was different. The other buildings had been like a holiday place, a luxurious beach hotel, with the high ceilings, gauzy curtains and big beds. This was more – scientific. As the door slid shut behind them, another opened in front, leading into a lift. They entered, Sally-Ann showed her palm, and the lift went down. Another door opened in front of them, and they stepped out on to a walkway – sleek, metal like an escalator.

They were moving along a corridor, basically.

There were ventilation shafts, he noticed, in the ceiling above his head.

A memory came to him – holes in the ceiling, in the roof, air and light coming in . . .

Paris! The underground canal!

We're not in a corridor, he thought – we're in a tunnel. We're going underground.

It was, he estimated, about fifteen minutes before the walkway led them into a second lift. Fifteen minutes at faster than walking pace, going in he didn't know what direction – but he did! They had come straight through the door in the rock, and the travelator had led straight off the lift, and it hadn't curved or turned . . . They were heading the way the door had faced, i.e. if he had his back aslant to the beach . . . kind of north-east. Good.

They went up a lot further in this lift. There were only

three stops, but the time between them was much longer than usual.

A tall building? With a few, very tall floors?

North-east. Hmm.

The lift stopped at its top stop. Doors slid open. Charlie and Sally-Ann slid out.

There was no travelator here. Just a smooth stone floor and smooth stone walls.

Bingo, thought Charlie. We're inside a mountain. Just as I thought. He was rather pleased with himself for having worked it out – but he remembered not to look as clever as he was.

'What a great place!' he said. 'Where are we?'

'We're going to the lab!' said Sally-Ann cheerfully. 'Just going to check a couple of things. It won't hurt!'

'My mummy works in a lab,' said Charlie, not because he wanted Sally-Ann to know, but because he wanted her to think of him as a sweet little boy who called his mum Mummy and wanted to tell irrelevant things to nice ladies.

It seemed to work. 'Does she, sweetie-pops?' she said.

When a woman you don't know calls you sweetie-pops, you can be pretty sure she's not thinking of you as an intelligent person. Good.

The lab, when they got to it, dispelled any remaining sense Charlie might have had of a beach hotel. It was bleak and sleek, stainless steel and glass, lined with VDUs and plasma screens, machines and technological units that

Charlie, despite his experience of his parents' labs, didn't recognize at all.

'Pop this on,' said the smiling Sally-Ann, handing him a pale green surgical gown. Charlie squinted at it. He didn't at all feel like popping it on. 'And look! Here's Dr Gascoigne!'

'Hello, Charlie,' said Dr Gascoigne, a large, calm-looking person with a greyish-purple face.

'What . . . Um . . .' said Charlie.

Dr Gascoigne gave a short smile.

'Nothing will hurt!' he said. Even he sounded like Sally-Ann.

And in the end, nothing did hurt. Charlie listened to the chat of the lab hands and the doctor and picked up that they were scanning his brain, reading his magnetism, resonating his radioactivity, X-raying him from head to foot and – which he especially didn't like – taking some of his blood for analysis.

They'll be checking my DNA, he thought. My genes. He wondered how long it would take them to work out that he had cat blood.

He wondered what he could do about it.

He thought, I don't have long. I must . . . I must . . . steal Sally-Ann's identity and go places I'm not allowed and . . . and . . . knock over my blood sample . . .

He felt tired after all the day's tests: all he had done, and all they had done to him.

He was glad when Sally-Ann gave him back his clothes and led him out into the corridor.

Walking back to the lift, she said, 'There, that wasn't too bad, was it?'

She's kind, he thought. She's kind but she's not herself. It's as if her real kindness has been wrapped up in some fake kindness. She's breathing the Sweet Air, obviously — maybe it's like an enchantment in a fairy tale, and she's really a nice woman underneath.

In which case she was a kind of prisoner too.

On the way to the lift they stopped for a moment at another room. It was, as Charlie had thought, carved out of the rock. Sally-Ann stepped in and exchanged a few words with a handsome, smartly dressed black woman sitting at a desk. She reminded Charlie of his Ghanaian aunties and their friends — busy, clever women, nice clothes, waste no time.

'Bring him in!' the woman said. 'Of course!'

Charlie stood in front of her. Her office was windowless — the only light came from a lamp hanging from the ceiling. Her desk was old-fashioned, made of wood. Her shelves were heavy with files.

'Charlie,' she said, and her voice sent a shiver up his back because it was a West African woman's voice, with the same timbre and accent as his grandma's, but overlaid with the Sally-Ann fake cheerfulness thing. The combination made him feel peculiar.

'Charlie, my name is Auntie Auntie. I am in charge of all the talented children here. I will be supervising your education and your health needs. If you have any problem, you must come to me. Every day will not be like today, with tests and exams and going to the lab. You will have fun here as well, and a chance to be friends with the other young people! The Corporacy wants you to make the most of yourself! You will see me again soon. Embrace your aspirations, Charlie! You are going to be happy here!'

'Right,' said Charlie. 'OK.' He looked at her. He wasn't sure what was expected of him.

So he smiled. The big fake smile.

She smiled it back.

Sally-Ann smiled it too.

All three stood there grinning like deluded idiots.

And then Charlie heard a dog bark, and he said, 'Oh! A dog!' and Auntie Auntie shot Sally-Ann a look, and Sally-Ann said quickly, 'Oh, yes, there are some animals,' and Charlie's train of thought shifted completely. Animals?

Sally-Ann ushered him towards the lift.

'Goodbye!' called Auntie Auntie.

Animals, thought Charlie. Sleep on it, he told himself. Talk to Sergei and Ninu.

It was still raining in the Gulf of Gonaïve. The heat and wet were unbearable. Suleiman had that morning announced that God wanted him to return to Morocco, so Aneba and

Magdalen had transferred on to Younus's ship, *El Baraka*. Younus wasn't happy, though – he was afraid she would start to rot. In fact, everybody felt as if everything was about to start to rot.

Edward had emailed King Boris charts and details of the neighbouring islands, and all the information about San Antonio he could muster. They had studied it, peering in turn at the tiny screen of the King's email phone, and formed their plan. It involved night rescue, swimming, inaccessible coastlines, risk . . . It was the best they could come up with.

The remaining question was, what would the others do while Aneba was away?

'Well,' said King Boris, 'let's remove ourselves from this dreadful place, and await the call. We don't have to sit around here while Aneba does his bit. Those animals need a run around and some nice meat to eat. As it happens, I have a friend living nearby who, I'm sure, would be delighted to offer us hospitality. We used to play cricket together. Shall I give him a ring?'

Magdalen was astonished. Hospitality? What an idea! But actually – what a nice idea.

She looked at Claudio. Claudio, of course, was very used to doing exactly what King Boris wanted.

'Is it safe?' asked Magdalen. 'I mean – the Lions, the Corporacy . . .'

'Oh, the Corporacy hate him, so that's all right . . . and

the Lions? Well, fifty years ago he might have wanted to shoot them, but he's calmed down a lot.'

They all looked at Aneba.

'As long as it is close, so you can come quickly when I need you,' he said. 'And if you are sure it is safe.'

King Boris took out his telephone. 'It's just north of here,' he said.

Aneba nodded.

King Boris was looking up a number.

'Shall I?' he said. 'He has plenty of room and is quite high up – well, he's the ruler – so we shouldn't have any trouble . . . I can vouch for him . . . hmm?'

'OK by me,' said Magdalen. King Boris had done right by Charlie before. The Lions weren't objecting, so *if* they understood humans, they trusted him too – and they'd been imprisoned in his palace. They couldn't all stay on *El Baraka* forever, and they certainly didn't want to stick around in Port-au-Prince.

'OK,' said Aneba.

'Marvellous,' said King Boris, with a moustache-twirling grin, pressing the number.

'Hello! *Hola!*' he cried. '*Hola! Fidel! . . . Sí, Boris! Estoy aquí! . . . Sí! Port-au-Prince! Vengo con mis amigos a tu casa! Dos de mis amigos son leones!* OK? *. . . Sí! . . . Leones! Sí! Gracias! Gracias! Ciao!*'

King Boris closed his phone. 'He's expecting us,' he said happily.

As they sailed back to Port-au-Prince a despondency settled over the ship. Aneba shaved and washed and oiled his skin. Now he put on the suit he had bought in Paris. Despite the heat he looked cool and elegant and ready to go.

He caught Magdalen's eye, and she grinned at him bravely. 'Bye then,' she said with a cheerfulness she did not feel.

A lurch indicated that they had reached the quay.

'I'll ring you,' he said. 'I'll be in touch all the time. You know where I am!'

'Yeah,' she said, and bit her lip.

'I'll find him,' he said.

'Yeah.'

'I'll call you – you know what to do.'

'Yeah.'

'He's a tough boy.'

'Yeah.'

'They won't harm him.'

'No.'

She turned away so that he wouldn't see her fear. Then she hurriedly gave him a huge hug, hiding her head in his chest. 'Off you go,' she mumbled. 'I love you.'

Shouldering his bag (telephone, clean shirts, several large and small bottles of liquid – he'd left some with Magdalen, for later), Aneba strode off down the grimy concrete quay towards the sad and dangerous market. He could see the shabby café where one of his new acquaintances was waiting to point out the lady from San Antonio. All he had to do was wait for her.

CHAPTER

FIFTEEN

When Charlie got back to his room, Ninu wasn't there. He looked for him (pretending to be fiddling with his toenails) and called him, but all he got was an answering mraowl from Sergei, still lurking under the shrubbery.

Sergei looked very upset.

'What is it?' asked Charlie.

Sergei blinked. 'You're not going to like this,' he said. For once he wasn't being sarcastic or sardonic or anything like that.

'What?' said Charlie. 'What's happened?'

'I couldn't do anything,' Sergei said, his voice choking up. 'He was just there, on the rock, over by the fountain. And this bliddy great bird – oh, Charlie . . .'

Charlie's skin started to crawl.

'I don't know, a bliddy great big eagle thing, just swooped down, and . . .'

No! Not little Ninu!

'It was twice my size. I ran at 'im, but he was gone already, I couldn't – I'm so sorry, Charlie . . .'

Ninu?

'He took him, Charlie. Just took 'im. I watched 'em fly away.'

No. No. Not little Ninu, who he had brought here; Ninu, who had gone down the Rat Network for him, who had sat so patiently for so long in his pocket; clever, brave, sweet Ninu, with his weird tongue and his googly eyes and his funny little hands . . .

Charlie was crying. He ran into the hut. Then out again, because he knew Sergei wouldn't come in with him.

He crawled under the beautiful bush and huddled in the dust, against the wooden wall of the hut, out of view of the spies. He clutched his knees and shook with the horror. Sergei, looking at him, felt a surge of love and sympathy. He cuddled up close to him, trying to get into his arms, on to his lap.

Charlie reached out his arm to hug Sergei, and he wept.

Rafi was in the vegetable farm, digging trenches. It was hard work and the sun was hot. Sweat and dust mingled, his bad shoulder ached, and blisters were coming up on his hands, but the air was sweet and Rafi wasn't thinking about anything much.

He leaned on his shovel and looked up into the bright, bright sky.

An eagle flew by, heading to the mountains, carrying

something in its claws. Not that Rafi noticed.

The overseer shouted at him to keep digging. Rafi wiped his sweaty forehead with his dusty arm and turned back to the trench.

Maccomo had fully intended to leave San Antonio as soon as he had his money. But somehow he hadn't got round to it yet. It was very pleasant, after all, and Capitaine Drutzel and the crew seemed in no hurry, so . . .

There was something he was meant to be doing . . . Well, it could wait.

Aneba sat at the unsteady tin café table by the quay in Port-au-Prince, sipping bad coffee and the Sweet-Air antidote, and watching. Three women in flip-flops and faded cotton dresses walked past with baskets; a child with a snotty nose; a priest in his robes; a skinny man in mechanic's overalls. He was amazed by their capacity to carry on normal human activities in this nightmarish place. The human spirit, he mused, is unconquerable.

Under his breath Aneba hummed the tune he hummed when he was doing nothing, the old Ghanaian tune, *Tuwe tuwe, mamuna tuwe tuwe* . . .

Auntie Auntie, stepping delicately across the muddied square, a clean and prosperous figure against the residue of storm and poverty, caught the tune on the breeze. I know that song, she thought, and looked around – and saw Aneba at about the same moment that he took his companion's nudge and saw her.

'Eh,' she said. 'God is merciful.' But before she could alert her two securityguys, Aneba stood up and approached her.

'Madame,' he said, holding out his hand in a relaxed and manly fashion. 'Please forgive me addressing you like this in the street when we have not been introduced . . .'

Auntie Auntie was rather surprised by this formality. She liked it.

'Hello, Professor,' she said.

'I'm glad of this opportunity to meet you, Madame,' Aneba continued, 'because as you know it can be complicated sometimes to make contact with the right people.'

'Indeed,' she said.

'And I would be interested to make contact with your personnel department . . .'

'No need for that,' she said with a smile.

One of her securityguys interrupted worriedly. 'But all applicants must go through Personnel, Madame,' he said. 'Security requires it! There is danger everywhere.'

'All aliens are suspect!' said the other one. 'If they're not with us, they're against us –'

'He has already been approved by Personnel,' said Auntie Auntie. 'Don't you recognize him?'

They stared.

'Well,' said Aneba, 'having previously been –'

She stopped him there. 'Perhaps you should come with me to San Antonio now,' she said.

'Perhaps,' Aneba replied. 'But perhaps first we should address the matter of my terms.'

Auntie Auntie raised an eyebrow.

'Terms?' she asked.

'And conditions,' Aneba said firmly.

'Ah,' she said thoughtfully. 'With a view to . . . cooperation?'

'With a view to embracing my aspirations,' said Aneba with a smile – *the* smile. The Aneba Ashanti full-on rising-sun-after-a-dark-winter *genuine* smile.

Auntie Auntie was dazzled.

The HCE, when he heard, couldn't have been happier. When Auntie Auntie brought Aneba in, the HCE clasped his hand, hugged him, slapped him manfully on the back. He agreed to his terms almost before Aneba could say what they were.

'My own laboratory . . .'

'Of course!'

'Professional independence . . . No one telling me what to do . . .'

'Of course!'

'My own phone . . .'

'Of course!'

'Long walks unaccompanied, to think clearly . . .'

'Of *course*!'

'My son must work with me . . .'

Not even a pause to acknowledge that they had his son. 'Of course!' cried the HCE.

Aneba betrayed nothing of his feelings.

'You understand that my wife does not share my change of heart,' he continued.

'I am disappointed,' said the HCE. 'But perhaps in time, with your loving support and encouragement . . .'

Aneba tried to look loving, supportive, encouraging and disappointed all at once. 'Let us hope so,' he said. Should he wipe away a manly tear? No, that would be too much. 'But in the meantime, working without her, it may take me a little longer . . .' he suggested.

'Of course!'

Aneba was thinking of the story of the sun and the wind, both trying to get a man to take his cloak off. The wind blew and blew, as cold as he could, but the man just pulled his cloak tighter round himself. The sun shone warmly and kindly: the man took the cloak off in moments. The HCE was shining at him, and yes, Aneba seemed to be offering up his cloak.

The HCE, for his part, was trusting that Corporacy life and the Sweet Air would soon persuade Aneba from any remaining inclinations towards independence. (But then the HCE did not know about the antidote – he had no need. As head of the Corporacy he might have wanted to protect himself from the Sweet Air, but the truth was far from that: he loved the Sweet Air as he loved everything else about the Corporacy, and lived in it with everybody else, because he thought it was right and good.)

In other words, each man sat there smiling at the other because each man thought he could outdo the other.

Magdalen knew Aneba would do his best, she knew it was right that she should remain behind . . . but she was nervous, she was jumpy. She was lonely. Charlie gone, Aneba gone, and her just stuck there in Fidel's balmy garden with nothing to contribute . . .

Some butterflies were flying in circles and settling on the dusty path.

She made a call.

'Mabel?'

'Yes! Hello, darling!'

'Where are you?'

'Well, we *were* heading for a summer season in New England, but the tour fell through so now we're headed to New Orleans – we're going up the Mississippi instead. All a bit last minute . . . What's the news on Charlie?'

'Listen, can you get some time off and come to Cuba – can you persuade Major Tib?'

'No way!'

'Try – please! Tell him it'll be worth it. Please. Anything you can do. Please! We need you!'

'Why?'

'I want to see you. I miss you. And – I think we've found Charlie. Aneba's gone to get him – I'm going a bit mad waiting . . . Anyway, you should be here. We might need help. OK, we need all the help we can get. Just . . . please.'

'Well,' said Mabel, surprised by the strength of her sister's plea. 'I don't know – I'll try.'

'Oh, I know you can't,' said Magdalen. 'I know you're contracted to Major Tib and you have bookings and everything and you can't just walk out on the Circus . . . It's not anything practical. I just wanted you to know I want you.'

'Thanks,' said Mabel. 'I – thanks.'

'Yeah. Yeah, I know. See you.'

Claudio, gazing from Fidel's veranda, had overheard part of this. He felt much the same helplessness that Magdalen felt.

English people like tea, he thought. I'll make her some tea.

At least it gave him something to do.

Charlie was still under the bush with Sergei when Sally-Ann came to him. He was no longer weeping, but his face was streaked with dust and tears, and his eyes were red and bruised-looking.

'Hey, Charlie!' she sang, from the terrace.

Sergei gave Charlie a strong look. Charlie scruffled Sergei's ears and stood up. 'I'll see you later,' he whispered.

'I'll be here,' said Sergei.

Charlie hurtled past Sally-Ann, shouting, 'Sorry – bathroom.' Once inside he washed his face and hands, splashed his head, shook himself down and stared into the mirror.

'I am Charlie,' he told his reflection. 'I am brave and I don't give up.'

Then he went to face his companion with a fake, Sweet-Air smile.

'Charlie!' she said. 'Got some good news for you! Guess what!'

Never had Charlie found it so hard to respond to Sally-Ann's ridiculous optimism. He forced a grin.

'What?' he said. It sounded completely fake. Because it was.

'Come with me and see!'

Charlie narrowly prevented himself from rolling his eyes. Instead he gritted his teeth. Grief had no place here – he had to hide it. He *had* to. Grit your teeth. Smile.

Tears sprang again behind his eyes.

Smile!

Sally-Ann took his hand and led him to the tram. They rode it as far as the lift entrance, entered the tunnel, and took the lift up inside the mountain. Charlie looked around and kept his eyes open. The more familiar he was with this place, the better.

Concentrating on that would help him to not think about . . . No, he wasn't going to think about that.

Again they went to the top floor; again along window-less stone corridors.

And then Sally-Ann held up her hand, a door slid back, and they were in a big office, with glass walls looking out over the sea, sunlight streaming in, sky and seabirds and craggy rock outside. Charlie gasped at the view.

'Hey, young fella!' said the HCE.

Charlie turned. 'Hey!' he said, Sweet-Air style.

'Great to have ya with us! Real glad to hear ya've been doin' well! Settlin' right in, I been informed!'

'Yessir!' said Charlie. It seemed like the kind of thing he was expected to say.

'I'm the HCE! That means the Head Chief Executive. Hey – you work hard, you never know: maybe some day *you* could be HCE too!'

'Golly gee, sir!' cried Charlie. Was he laying it on too thick? No, they looked pleased.

'Meantime, boy, we got another job for ya. Important job only you can do – and *make sure you do it right.*'

It was then that Aneba was brought in from an adjoining room.

Charlie's jaw dropped.

Aneba's eyes lit up.

They both knew exactly how important this moment was, and how important it was that they say the right thing.

'Golly gee, Daddy!' cried Charlie. He held out his hand to shake.

'And how's my best little boyo, then?' said Aneba, taking it, and shaking it, and smiling a fake smile.

Each was thinking the exact same thing. Is his head clear? Has the Sweet Air got him?

And each could see, beneath the fake chummy greeting, the artificial smile and the stupid words, the love and joy and pure relief of being together at last. At last, something had gone right.

CHAPTER
SIXTEEN

They were shown the new lab that was to be theirs. They grinned at each other, but couldn't talk freely.

They were shown Aneba's hut – not far from Charlie's. They grinned, but couldn't talk.

They were introduced to Aneba's Assigned Assistant, a thin young man called Alex. Were they never going to be able to talk?

Finally, 'Leave us alone together,' Aneba demanded grandly.

Alex and Sally-Ann looked doubtful.

'It's my terms,' said Aneba earnestly. 'You know the HCE agreed. I can't think and work properly when people are looking over my shoulder. If I can't think and work, I will never produce the results that the Corporacy wants from me – I will never achieve my aspirations . . .'

He looked positively sad. Sally-Ann and Alex looked sad too. They quite understood. They backed off. Not very far, though.

Charlie and Aneba went to Charlie's hut and sat outside, by the bush.

'How's Mum?' Charlie asked. Then the words started falling out of him. He spoke in Twi to confuse any eaves-droppers. Quickly and quietly he told Aneba about the commchip system: 'They can hear everything and talk to each other wherever they are – I'm not sure if there are cameras in there too, and if pictures go back to the secu-rity centre . . . Anyway even if there's no one with us, we're still overlooked and overheard by the general security cam-eras. It's best to talk outside, and even so pretend we're just laughing and telling stories . . .' He gave an inane little giggle, and pointed to the horizon as if he were admiring the view.

Aneba followed his son's finger, and shaded his eyes. 'Is that the chip in the skin under the ear?' he asked.

'Yeah,' said Charlie.

'I'm assuming you don't have one.'

'Nope – I'm still too small.'

'They're planning to give me one,' said Aneba, still gazing out to sea. 'Tomorrow, they said . . . so we must go before they do, or they'll be able to track us and really eavesdrop . . . But how come you're clear-headed, Charlie? I've got the antidote, but why isn't the Air affecting you?'

'Cat blood, we think . . .'

'Cat blood! How interesting – but who's *we*?'

'Sergei!' said Charlie. 'He's – where is he?'

He was right there. He coiled his tail at Aneba in greeting. Aneba smiled. He was glad his son hadn't been all alone.

'And Ninu . . . but . . .'

Charlie told his dad about Ninu. Aneba held him tight.

'So listen,' said Aneba. 'Magdalen, King Boris, Claudio and two of the Lions are here –'

'What?' squeaked Charlie. He was so surprised, he almost forgot to disguise his words. Realizing, he laughed loudly. Then started almost getting hysterical. This was too much. First Ninu, then Dad, now everybody else . . .

'So we'll get you off the island,' said Aneba.

'Off the island,' said Charlie, and he blinked.

It was just after dusk, as dinner was being served, that a shadow loomed out of the shade of evening, and landed on the beach near Charlie's hut.

'What the heck's that?' cried Aneba, but Charlie shushed him with a look and, yawning and stretching, wandered over towards the shape.

It was a bird.

It was the eagle.

'What!' shouted Charlie. 'You – you –!' He looked around for a rock, a stick, something to hit it with or throw at it, this murderous bird, this thieving friend-killer, this –

'Charlie! Stop it!' came a tiny voice.

Charlie stopped.

He could see nothing.

The eagle arced.

Charlie looked round.

'I'm here,' said the voice plaintively. 'Come on, Charlie, I *am* a chameleon.'

He was purply grey, in the shadow under the eagle's great feathery breast.

Ninu! Was it?

'I'm all right!' Ninu said. 'He's my friend!'

Charlie gasped. He wanted to cry out and dance around. Ninu! He crunched his teeth tightly together so that no squeal of joy should give him away, shook his head madly like a dervish and then he threw himself down on the sand, on his back. 'Dad!' he said loudly. 'Dad! Come and look at the stars! They're fab!'

Aneba came out. Lay down.

'Watch it!' squeaked a little voice.

Aneba jumped. 'What's that?' he said, surprised, but remembering he had to keep his voice down.

Charlie giggled. Ninu was stepping delicately on to his tummy and it tickled.

'Dad, Ninu, Ninu, my dad.'

'But you're dead,' said Aneba.

'No, I'm not,' said Ninu.

Charlie couldn't stop grinning. Not dead!

'And you're talking,' said Aneba.

'Yes,' said Ninu. 'And listen, I don't mean to be rude,

but, um, could you get used to it really quickly because I think there's quite a lot to do . . .'

Aneba was goggling, his mouth going like a goldfish's.

'Come on, Dad, you're a scientist, you know the world is full of wonders,' said Charlie.

'Er, yeah,' said Aneba. He was still goggling, though.

'So what happened?' said Charlie, eyeing the eagle.

'I, um, explained to my, um, chauffeur, that I might be more useful if I wasn't lunch,' said Ninu. 'Like most big animals, he wasn't used to being talked to by a snack, so he put me down and we had a chat. He's great and he knows all kinds of things . . .' Here he broke off and addressed the eagle briefly.

Aneba was beside himself with excitement.

'Can he talk to anyone?' he said. 'To everyone?'

'Yeah,' said Charlie.

But Ninu was continuing. 'He showed me how these humans are ruining the island,' he said. 'He sees it all because his nest is right at the top of the mountains. He has lived here many years. He knew the island before these ones came, he knows where they keep the animals prisoner, and where their ships come and go, and where they built their tunnels, and where their poison air comes from –'

'Really?' said Aneba. 'Where?'

Ninu translated. The eagle wanted to know why Aneba wanted to know. Aneba, hardly believing that he was negotiating with an eagle through a chameleon, said,

'Because I have the antidote – I could perhaps feed it through the system . . .'

The eagle lowered its fantastic brows and lifted its feathered shoulders.

'He wants to know your plans,' said Ninu. 'He has no time for humans.'

'Tell him,' said Aneba, 'that Charlie and I intend to . . . to . . .'

'To end the reign of these humans,' said Charlie. 'To end the Sweet Air, and free the animals, and liberate the people, and make it all right again.'

He found himself staring at Aneba. Was that what they were going to do?

Aneba was staring back.

'Yes?' asked Charlie.

'How do we liberate the people?' asked Aneba. There was something doubtful in his tone, but Charlie didn't have time to notice it.

'I'm not sure yet,' said Charlie. 'But – well, we have to do something with them . . .'

The eagle was giving them his piercing look.

Ninu said, 'He wants to know, will the humans go away?'

'Some of them, yes,' said Charlie.

'The evil ones?'

Charlie found it hard to believe that anyone was really evil. But he knew evil existed. How could that make sense?

'Yes,' he said. Now was a time for decision, not for philosophizing. He'd come back to that later.

The eagle lifted his head and stared out into the darkness over the sea.

'He says he will tell us where the Sweet Air comes from,' said Ninu. 'And where the animals are kept. He says he will help.'

That night, Charlie invited the other kids to come and watch telly with him.

'OK,' they said, with empty smiles.

They watched *The Simpsons*, smiling blankly all the way through and laughing at the wrong bits. It made Charlie really angry to see them out of kilter like that. 'I'll get them back,' he said to himself, through clenched teeth. 'I'll get them all back, and then I'll get them out of here.' He offered them drinks. They all drank the sugary fizz from the fridge without noticing the drops from his dad's bottle that Charlie had added.

By the time they were watching their third episode, Seventeen was giggling and making comments, the Starlets' keeper had started to sing along with the theme tune and Charlie was beginning to think there was hope. But then Sally-Ann arrived to say they had used up all the time allocated for social community integration that night, and that it wasn't all right to hang out now without advance permission, so they had to return to their rest and privacy units. Charlie looked around, wanting to catch someone's eye for a giggle at this ludicrous phrase, but the others just quietly filed out.

The drops will work, he told himself. They were starting to.

Early the next morning, Aneba took a long walk to clear his mind for the day ahead. The HCE was not nervous about this: the Sweet Air would be doing its thing, and anyway, Dr Ashanti had embraced Corporacy aspirations! No one could hold out for long. Soon – today! – he would be working away on that asthma cure, and the Corporacy would own all the rights to it. No, the HCE didn't mind him going for a walk. Where could he go, after all?

Better get his commchip in soon, though.

Aneba went exactly where the eagle had told him to go. It was a low concrete hut, with a magnetism-based security system on it that Aneba was able to dismantle quite swiftly because he had, as a younger man, worked on the prototype. Once inside, he took a quick look at the relatively simple air-conditioning system that had been distributing the Sweet Air across the island, and made a few minor changes.

'Cunning,' he said, noticing that the Sweet-Air molecules had been chemically weighted, to prevent them all from just blowing away across the sea.

He sipped again from his personal supply of antidote,

keeping a small puddle of it in his mouth. The Sweet Air was strong here, and he didn't want to be overwhelmed when he disconnected the supply to the distribution system.

Right. That would be the Sweet-Air tank, there was the supply pipe – he cut straight through the heavy black rubber with his big knife, breathing through his mouth. Swiftly he poured some of the antidote into the air tank as well, and sealed it up, jamming the mechanism, in case anybody might try to reconnect it later. There.

It didn't take long to reconnect the distribution pipe to his largest bottle of antidote. He fixed the join with rubberized putty. Neither the seal nor the bottle itself would last very long, but for a while it would cover the island and, after that, fresh air and sea breezes would kick in, and the effects of the Sweet Air would wear off anyway.

'That should do for now,' he said. 'And with any luck there won't be any later.'

That afternoon, Charlie (with the happy reassuring weight of Ninu in his pocket again) was summoned to the new lab in the mountain sector. For a moment, when he had first seen it, Aneba's heart had lifted – so much equipment! So new! He would have been delighted, under other circumstances, to have settled down to work in this wonderful lab.

'If only,' he had said. 'If only . . .'

But this afternoon he looked grim. As he turned his head, Charlie saw why.

On his neck, beneath his ear, was a clean white patch of gauze. A tiny spot of blood, red and fresh-looking, seeped at the centre.

It was very difficult for Charlie to regain his composure and congratulate his dad on being accepted as a full member of the Corporacy Community. But he did it.

'That's great, Dad!' he said, as convincingly as he could. He felt sick inside. 'Your commchip! Is it working yet? Wow! Now you can talk to everybody all the time!'

'No, it's not connected yet,' Aneba said. 'They'll turn it on later – not sure when, but probably today. And in the meantime Alex is here with us.'

Charlie had known it would happen, but it made him miserable. He felt as if he and his father would never again be alone together.

'So we'd better get down to work, eh, Charlie? Because they'll be needing you for your own testing soon – I won't have you as my assistant forever, you know.'

'Yes, of course,' said Charlie. 'Let's get on then . . . We need to see the animals. We'll need to test the results on them,' he said grandly. 'Won't we, Dad?'

'Yes, of course,' said Aneba. 'Take us there, please,' he said to Alex.

Alex, whose commchip was being monitored full-time so that the HCE could see what Aneba was up to in the lab, was not sure how to respond, but the answer came immediately from the HCE – yes, Dr Ashanti could be taken to the animals. How glad the HCE was that Ashanti wasn't one of these inconvenient animal rights types. In fact, hearing that he was going to be testing on animals made the HCE feel more confident than ever in his decision to give Dr Ashanti some leeway and freedom in his work. He was relieved now that they'd got his commchip in place, but it looked like he was the Right Type – the Corporacy Type – after all.

This was, of course, exactly what Aneba wanted him to think.

The Animal Farm was high, high up on the mountain: man-made caves as animal sheds; man-made terraces serving as fields and pens, some of them arched with wire netting as aviaries. The breeze kept it cool, it was clean, the food was OK, but it couldn't have been more of a prison. The only way to or from it was by air, or through the Corporacy's tunnel. The animals sat there, looking out over the beautiful sea, sniffing the wind, hoping that today was not their day to be taken to the lab. And that was it.

Sergei was already there. The eagle had given him a lift and dropped him in one of the stalls. When Charlie and Aneba arrived, he was deep in conversation with another cat.

Charlie, wary as ever of Alex's commchip and the possibility of cameras, knelt down and went, 'Here, kitty kitty,'

in a babyish way. It was kind of pointless, given that the
Corporacy knew he could talk to cats, but it was so much
part of his nature to be discreet about his Catspeaking –
and to conceal whatever he could from the Corporacy –
that he did it automatically.

Kneeling, he got a shock.

The cat Sergei introduced him to – her name was Jungko
– was small and silky and very beautiful, like the Burmese
cats Charlie had seen in London. That was not so unusual.
What stopped him short was her tail: at the end, it was
forked.

She bowed gently to Charlie and addressed him in a
curious form of Cat, which, though he could understand
it, he recognized was quite different from what he was accustomed to. It was like the way Petra's mother used to talk
– Petra was half Oriental.

'*Konichiwa*,' she said. 'We are glad to see you here. Your
friend has been telling us about the world outside. Can you
help us?'

Behind her were stall after stall of animals. Immediately
to her left, three extraordinary little creatures looked up
hopefully. They were bald and silky, with wrinkled skin pat-
terned pink and black, slitty eyes and huge ears. They looked
like space creatures.

'We're Sphynx kittens,' one said. 'Apparently they want
our baldness. They can have it! But when can we go home?'

Beyond them was another peculiar cat with pale green

eyes, velvety rippled fur like a baby lamb's, and ears almost as big, if not so intergalactic.

'I'm John,' he said. 'I'm a Devon rex. I can't think why they'd want me. I've been trying to work it out, and perhaps it's because we're not very allergenic in my family – I don't know. I don't know what they're up to. I've not been here long.' He drew to a halt, embarrassed to have said so much. 'Not like . . .' He glanced towards a pen on its own, further away, where what looked like a very furry bundle lay in a heap.

Charlie went up to it.

At one end, one eye opened.

'Hello,' said Charlie, and sneezed.

It was a cat – the fluffiest, furriest cat Charlie had ever seen. Even though it wasn't moving, downy lint seemed to float off it of its own accord.

'Yeah, sorry,' the cat muttered. 'Everybody's allergic to me. You'd better move away. You asthmatic? Yeah – just go away, would you? It's not my fault . . . I don't want to cause trouble . . .'

Charlie moved away, and took a puff of his inhaler just in case. He was thinking.

Further down the line another cat spoke, the colour of crème caramel, with blue eyes. 'My name is Marta,' she said. 'I am Espanish. In my family we make nests in bamboo.' Then she too was covered with fear and shyness, and quickly curled up and hid her nose under her paws.

A long-legged, splay-footed reptile spoke up. 'I walk on water!' he said. 'I know, because they call me the Jesus Lizard. I know that's why they wanted me.'

A smaller, dark lizard beside him said simply, 'I can go in fire.'

Ninu, fascinated, told Charlie.

Across from the cats were stalls full of dogs. Charlie, with a determined look on his face, went over to them and had Ninu translate. Though Ninu was nervous, he knew he had to oblige.

First up was a dark, curly dog with bright eyes. 'My name is Blue,' he said. 'My family were originally fishermen's dogs in Portugal, but we've been in California for a while now. I was taken from my place by the ocean there. My human will be sad without me . . .'

'Ask him why he was taken – does he know?' whispered Charlie to Ninu.

'Webbed feet,' said Blue mournfully. 'Useful webbed feet. They think they are God! Making animals! Changing animals! Doesn't the world already have enough beautiful animals? And do the humans look after the ones there are?'

'Have they made any yet?' Charlie asked urgently.

'They made the ones like your friend,' said Jungko.

Sergei looked around at the animals, embarrassed, shy, sad.

'I have been here a long time,' Jungko continued. She glanced at the very fluffy cat. 'They found the allergenic gene and made all the Allergenie cats and sent them all round the world. And they put Allergenie babies in kidnapped cats and then sent them back where they came from.'

'That's likely what happened to me,' murmured Sergei. 'I know my dad thought I was his.' He looked suddenly hurt, at the idea of not being his dad's. He too glanced at the fluffy cat, but it had turned its back on the proceedings.

'I saw it,' Jungko continued. 'I heard them. They think we're stupid and dumb, but we're not – we're just private and quiet. We know what they're doing. And I knew an Allergenie would come back one day.' She gave Sergei a proud look.

'They're over there,' whispered Marta to Sergei, peeping towards a stall to her left.

Slowly, Sergei paced over in that direction. His pupils were little black slits in his milky blue eyes. Reaching the rail, he dipped his head and called softly.

A bundle of kittens, skinny little things, rolled and padded and bustled towards him. Behind them was a rank of tired-looking females, and beyond them more kittens, and more females, and more kittens.

''Ello,' he said.

The kittens squeaked and mewed at him. He padded at them gently between the bars.

''Ello, you lot,' he murmured. Then turned and looked at Charlie.

And Charlie turned and looked at Aneba.

And Aneba looked around at all the animals, the cats and dogs and birds and lizards. And back at Charlie.

'OK,' Charlie said. 'Time to get this show on the road.'

'Well, OK,' said Alex. All he had seen was a kid enjoying the zoo. 'What do you need? They're at your disposal, the HCE said. Obviously he'd prefer you not to, er, finally render any of them, er, finished, as they are being used for ongoing research . . .'

'Alex,' said Aneba, 'drink a little of this, go and stand over there by the cliff, and breathe deeply. I'll call you when I've finished looking around.' He handed him the small anti-dote bottle.

'Oh – OK,' said Alex, who had been feeling a little odd since that morning anyway – a little less certain about everything than he usually did – and was glad of the chance just to stand and gaze out to sea. Goodness, it was beautiful. He took a sip from the bottle. The sea reminded him of . . . of . . . something. How strange – he hadn't felt this kind of sweet sadness for he didn't know how long. What was it called? Nostalgia! That's right. What a lovely word. How had he ever forgotten it?

Charlie was whispering to Ninu, 'Listen, this may do your head in but we're relying on you. Who here, among all these animals, has any idea how we can bring this empire down? Any weakness, any –' The phrase *Achilles' heel* sprang to his mind. 'Can you find out, and report back? Quickly now.'

Ninu scurried around the stalls, asking, listening, nodding his frilled head and swivelling his eyes from speaker to speaker. His brain hummed with the different languages.

Charlie addressed the cats.

'Jungko will think of something,' said Marta quietly. 'The Japanese fork-tail cats always had very strong magic.'

Jungko said, 'We are not demons any more, Marta – we are as powerless as everyone.'

Something in that phrase made Charlie think. *As powerless as everyone.*

An image came to him: Sigi Lucidi with all his children climbing and leaping on him, him holding them up. Pirouette swinging between trapezes, being caught and thrown by the other trapeze artistes. The acrobats, tumbling together. Sara and Tara, speaking at the same time. The clowns, catching each other when they fell. The band playing, linking everybody through the music, the rhythm, the timing, the mood. The creaking, wheezy parts of the Calliope, working together to make the fabulous racket that told the whole world that the Circus was in town, the Lions, leaping in their array, fighting off Rafi, being a gang, a pride. The whole team of the Circus.

'We're not powerless,' he said quickly. 'We're only powerless when we're alone. We're not powerless when we have each other and we talk to each other and do things together . . . DAD!' he shouted.

Aneba turned. 'What?' he called.

'I know what to do!' shouted Charlie. 'We have to take everybody, Dad, don't we? So what we should do is —'

Aneba was silent. The look on his face stopped Charlie in mid-flow.

Charlie looked at him expectantly. 'What is it, Dad?' he asked.

Aneba drew away from the animals. He'd suspected Charlie was thinking this. But . . . but . . . he couldn't let his son build up hopes that could never be fulfilled. He couldn't let him believe something that wasn't true. How could they possibly take all these animals from the island? Of course they couldn't — the idea was lunacy.

But how could he possibly tell his son that they had to save themselves and leave the others? That it was quite likely they wouldn't even be able to save themselves? That in a situation this dangerous any 'others' were just irrelevant?

He tried to move his mouth, but words wouldn't come.

'Charlie,' said Aneba finally, turning away and drawing his son with him.

'What?' insisted Charlie. He wasn't getting it.

'If we try to save everybody,' said Aneba, in a tight voice, 'we will none of us escape.'

'We might,' said Charlie cheerfully. 'It's worth a punt.'

'No,' said Aneba. He thought of the animals in the pens behind him. He thought of the other children Charlie had told him about. It wasn't his fault he couldn't save them all. He really really wished he could — but he knew that it wasn't possible. Damn it, would the boy not understand? This wasn't a shameful choice – it was survival, reality, responsibility.

'It's you and me, Charlie,' he said softly. 'Otherwise we don't have a chance.'

'But what about Seventeen and Twenty-One?' said Charlie. He really *didn't* understand. 'And the Starlets, and all these guys . . .' He gestured towards the animals. 'And Rafi . . .'

If his dad was surprised to hear Charlie show concern for Rafi, he didn't mention it. He just said, 'It's not possible. I'm really sorry, but it's just you and me.'

Charlie stared at his father. He was blinking, but his stare was steady. Aneba felt it like a shaft of flaming ice.

'Then it's just you, Dad,' said Charlie. His voice was hard. 'Because I've got some responsibilities here.' He reached out his hand and scratched Sergei between the ears, still giving Aneba that steady gaze. Then he turned suddenly and called to Ninu in Cat. The chameleon scurried over and took up his place in Charlie's pocket.

'See you back there,' Charlie said to Sergei. The eagle inclined his head, and Sergei braced himself for the flight home. Then, without a glance at his father, Charlie strode away towards the corridors and the lift.

The animals called out as he went. He could only understand the cats, but the message was clear: 'See you soon,

Charlie! Come back soon! We'll do whatever we can! We're relying on you!'

Aneba was calling to him too: 'Charlie – neither of us can do anything without the other!'

And then Alex was calling: 'Um – wait, please! Wait! You can't go back on your own! Please wait!'

Great, thought Charlie as he strode furiously down the corridor. Everyone's depending on us, and my dad's lost his nerve. So now everyone's depending on *me* . . . all these people, all these animals, it's all down to me. Thanks, Dad. Thanks very much.

But he was more than angry. He was hurt and desperately disappointed. His dad! Selfish and cowardly!

Charlie was ashamed of his dad.

CHAPTER
SEVENTEEN

Sally-Ann felt peculiar. There was a coolness in her mind, an edge. Her legs felt stronger than usual, and her sight kept flickering as if it were refocusing. In fact, her whole self felt as if it were refocusing.

This was inconvenient because she was having a serious conversation with Auntie Auntie about why the children were all so lively and naughty today. Jake Yeboa had jumped up in the middle of a lecture on the International Benefits of Corporacy Life and announced that he'd much rather be playing football, and not only all the boys but the girl twins too had started to laugh. Come to think of it, it was rather funny – after all, it was their footballing skills that these boys had come here to use . . .

She found herself saying this to Auntie Auntie.

Auntie Auntie hadn't been feeling herself at all. She hadn't wanted a cigarette with her morning coffee, and her coffee had been too sweet even though it was just as she usually had it. Plus her feet hurt at lunchtime, and she'd felt glad of it because she would enjoy putting them up on her desk.

Now, when Sally-Ann spoke of the boys having 'come here', for a moment, the thought of how they had arrived crossed her mind.

They had arrived in a ship from Africa against their will, in exchange for money, so that other people could profit from their strength and skill.

In a moment the thought was gone again, but it bothered her for the rest of the day – a thought that had escaped. She knew, somewhere in her mind, that she had to think that thought again, and think it through.

One of the securityguys at the harbour fell asleep. Seventeen's Assigned Companion got so embarrassed to see him like this that she got the giggles, whereupon Twenty-One's Assigned Companion started to tease her about fancying him. Then he woke up and blushed. How odd! They didn't normally behave like this. At least . . .

Two of them started to wonder what normal was.

In his room, Maccomo woke up. How long had he been napping? He had a strong urge for the Lionmedicine, which he hadn't wanted for weeks. Where was he anyway? And why did his head feel cool? He shouldn't be hanging around here – he had a lot to do. He'd got his money and disposed of the cargo – he should be on his way.

Rafi was in the fields. All through the day his fury had been building up. What was he doing here? How long had they had him doing this humiliating work? Who did this guy think he was, bossing him about? And why on earth had he,

Rafi, been putting up with it? I'm gonna clock 'im, he thought. He certainly wasn't going to put up with it any longer.

Charlie was filled with determination and energy, focused. Marching back from the lab, ignoring his dad, ignoring Alex, and ignoring the animals' voices running around in his mind, he had had a realization that had scared the daylights out of him.

He knew now what he was dealing with. Finally, he had worked it out.

The animals had all spoken of their special talents, their skills and idiosyncrasies. They had known, as if it went without saying, why they had been stolen: for their talents – like the children. And the only concrete result of whatever 'research' the Corporacy was doing with these animals was the Allergenies. They'd used the very fluffy allergenic cat to create the Allergenies, to increase the amount of medicine they could sell . . .

So what were they going to do with the other animals? Make fork-tailed web-footed bald non-allergenic mice that build nests in bamboo, walk on water and can go in fire?

How would they make money from that?

And what were they going to do with the children?

Make quick-fingered children? Football stars? Cat-speakers?

Web-footed children?

Children who can go in fire?

Quick-fingered cats?

He didn't even want to begin to think about it. 'I'd like two hundred quick-fingered children, please, to work the looms in my carpet factory . . .' 'I need twelve centre forwards, top of the range . . .' 'A gang of bald fireproof children to work in my furnaces, please . . .'

And Catspeaking? 'We need someone to devise a campaign to explain to the Wild Lions why they'd all be much happier in a zoo, so we can have their land and dig for oil.'

And why were they stealing Poor World children? Did they think they wouldn't be missed? Or that they'd only be missed by people with no power to get them back?

Charlie imagined Seventeen and Twenty-One's mum. The Starlets' mums.

He remembered Primo, created by science, without any kind of family.

He remembered how the cats in Venice had treated the Allergenies, despising them and hating them.

No way. No way, no way, no way was this going to happen.

OK, it was all down to him. Fine. He would deal with it. That's what difficulties are for. Dealing with. He, Charlie, was going to bring down this whole stinking notion.

And even if Dad weren't being cowardly and selfish, he had his commchip now, so he was a security risk. And anyway, Charlie had an idea – a very good one. Which he had been about to tell his dad, only his dad wouldn't listen. No, Charlie was better off just sticking with Sergei and Ninu. Humans – especially grown-ups – were nothing but trouble.

'OK,' he said to Ninu, back in his room. 'Stand there.' He positioned Ninu by the telly screen. 'Anything?'

The telly was on, loud. It helped disguise what they were saying – Sally-Ann was out on the terrace. And it – well, it was their experiment.

'Anything?' asked Charlie again.

Ninu was concentrating hard.

'Change channels,' he said.

Charlie flicked the remote.

Ninu dipped his eyes in thought.

'Is the mechanism of the telly in the screen?' he asked.

'Oh! Good thinking. No, it's in that console.' Charlie pointed to a panel on the wall where the controls for the windows, the AC, the heating and the TV were.

Ninu pattered over to it.

'Ah!' he said. 'Whoa!'

'Yes?' said Charlie eagerly.

'Change the channel,' said Ninu in concentration. 'Whoa! Well – well, I think . . . Yes! There's something beneath . . . Hmmmm . . .'

Charlie whooped.

Then he stuck his head outside.

'Sally-Ann,' he asked innocently and pleasantly, 'might I go and do a bit of work in the schoolroom? I'd like to look some stuff up on the computer!'

'What, now?' said Sally-Ann. 'You are eager. OK, then.'

She was a bit annoyed to be disturbed, to tell the truth. The feeling was not familiar to her. Or at least it was – from long ago. Annoyed! She hadn't felt annoyed since goodness knew when.

Aneba was in the forest, wandering around innocently, making a phone call. He was aware it was probably being monitored – his commchip may well have been activated by now, and anyway phone calls are always easy to listen in on. He felt dreadful about Charlie. But he knew he was right and he had to carry on the plan with Magdalen as if nothing had changed.

'Darling,' he said. 'Darling, please talk to me, don't be angry with me.'

Magdalen was delighted to hear his voice. Her heart leapt, but her voice gave nothing away.

'I'm not angry, darling, just disappointed,' she said. 'I know you're doing what you think is right. It's just that I don't agree with you.'

'I've been thinking,' Aneba said. 'You should give it a try. They're treating me really well. Charlie's working with me . . . And they would be so happy for you to come too. I think you should come over and just judge for yourself how things are. It's not like last time. The facilities are wonderful. There's this great lab up in the mountains, the air is great and no one is breathing down my neck telling me what to do. It's all very free and easy, and I think it will get easier. I really think you should come soon. Why not tonight? Just set off and I'm sure we could send someone to meet you at sea . . . No, of course you couldn't make it so quickly . . .'

'Well, of course not, darling, the journey itself would take much longer, plus I'd have to prepare. Plus – plus I don't want to, Aneba! After what they did to us before!'

'We have to get over that, darling. We have to deal with reality and move on,' Aneba said. 'I really wish you'd think seriously about coming. I love you.'

'I love you too,' she said.

'Think about it,' he said. 'I'll ring you later.'

So now she knew that the Sweet Air was gone, the lab was in the mountains and she was to come tonight with the boat and someone would meet her.

Oh, lord, but who? Aneba asked himself. Without Charlie and Ninu to arrange it, how could he send someone?

Magdalen, as she put away her phone, called to King Boris, who was drinking beer with his friend across the rather grand sitting room.

'That was him!' she cried.

'And?' cried King Boris, sitting upright and raising his bushy eyebrows.

'And we must go tonight, someone will meet us at sea.'

'Tonight!' said King Boris. 'Is that OK, Fidel?'

'Sooner the better,' said King Boris's friend, an old but strong-looking man in a beret, with a rather fine beard. 'My ship awaits.'

Magdalen, Boris and Claudio had been intending to use *El Baraka*, but Fidel, on hearing their plans, had insisted that they use his ship *El Teflon*, an experimental vessel that was, in theory, undetectable by modern security systems. 'It's good to make a test run,' he said. His crew would accompany them, of course, and a small flotilla of warships would back them up. Magdalen had thought about protesting, but then realized that actually she would be very glad to have back-up.

Fidel looked at his watch. 'You can leave in two hours, catch the tide, be there soon after dusk. Their north coast is difficult, but there are some little harbours possible, and if you will have a guide, you will find. Are Lions going?'

'Oh yes,' said Magdalen.

Fidel looked sad. He had enjoyed having Lions prowling his mansion.

Magdalen went to tell Claudio and the Lions.

She wished she had more information.

She hoped Aneba knew what he was doing.

*

In the schoolroom, Sally-Ann started to draw mermaids on the blackboard. Charlie smiled. He had been right, he was sure – she was a nice woman underneath, and now that the Sweet Air was wearing off, her true niceness was coming through.

While she was occupied, Charlie quickly turned on one of the student computers and logged on to it. Then Ninu crept out of his pocket and lay down carefully on top of the hard drive. He tilted his head as if he were listening.

He *was* listening.

Charlie looked at him expectantly.

Ninu was concentrating hard.

Suddenly he gave Charlie a very intense look and started swivelling his eyes wildly. Charlie glanced over his shoulder at Sally-Ann. Why couldn't she just go away?

Charlie bent his head to Ninu, and Ninu whispered to him. Charlie's face registered first delight, then satisfaction, then concern, then understanding, then – finally – determination.

'So be it,' he said, and shut down the computer.

'Finished already?' said Sally-Ann. 'Shame – I was having fun up here.'

'Well, you keep going!' Charlie said. 'I'm just going back to my room anyway. Go on! Don't mind me.'

'Do you know, I think I will,' said Sally-Ann. 'I'll see you later for dinner. Shall we go to the dining hall?'

'Yeah, let's,' said Charlie. 'Be nice to see the others.'

He smiled at her. She smiled at him. Normal smiles. No exclamation marks.

It was starting.

The Lions, though they did not particularly like boats, were extremely happy to be boarding *El Teflon*. They had been afraid that they would be kept in luxury again, in a luxurious prison, far from the action and prevented by humans from doing anything.

'Land ahoy!' shouted Elsina. 'Or rather, sea ahoy! Don't worry, Charlie, we're coming to get you!'

'They're a bit jumpy tonight, aren't they?' Magdalen asked Claudio.

'Maybe they wanted to sleep,' he replied. 'Or maybe they're hungry.'

Together they stared at Elsina and the Young Lion with a complete lack of understanding.

'Dingbats,' said the Young Lion contemptuously. 'They don't even know what they're going to do when they get there! They don't even know where they're going!'

The Lions, of course, knew exactly what they would do. They would catch Charlie's scent, find him, maul his enemies, fly like the wind with him on their backs and then – well yes, here the humans would be useful – deliver him safely to the boat.

*

The dining hall that night was positively rowdy. The Starlets were going stir-crazy – they were used to training for hours every day, and all this schoolwork was doing their heads in. Soon enough they were throwing food at one another. Seventeen and Twenty-One rolled their eyes.

Charlie, sitting between them, took advantage of the mayhem to whisper. 'Girls,' he said. 'Are you yourselves again?'

'So did it happen to you too?' whispered Seventeen. 'Wasn't it peculiar? Did you notice it happening? We didn't! And now it has gone!'

'Good,' said Charlie. 'So – shall we escape?'

They turned to him in amazement.

'There is a plan,' he said quietly. 'Tell the boys if you think they're back from – you know – that stupid mood we were put in.' (He didn't say he hadn't been in the stupid mood – he wanted to keep it simple.) 'It's happening tonight. You'll notice! Be up and alert, later on.'

'Yes, we will,' they said seriously, and their eyes were as big as when he had first seen them in the slave dungeon.

The night was dark and the ship invisible. The Lions lay quietly, breathing soft as the invisible prow nosed through the dim waves, surrounded by its invisible forcefields off which sound, light, radar, radio, magnetism and sonar bounced and broke up and re-formed, giving nothing away. She was a small smooth shape of nothing in the night. Every now and then the Lions heard a splash within her fields, but then the sound was broken up by Fidel's wave disrupters. Nothing nosed through the night, Cuba behind, San Antonio ahead. The moon shone down on nothing.

After dinner, Charlie announced that he and Aneba were going back up to the lab because Aneba wanted to get on with his work. In fact, all Aneba wanted to do was sort out a messenger to meet the ship – but that meant talking to Charlie, and as Charlie wasn't talking to him, that meant going where Charlie went and doing what Charlie wanted to do, until he did agree to talk to him, and the sooner the better.

'Yes, I just want to get started properly,' said Aneba.

Well, ain't that something! thought the HCE, observing. Ain't he keen after all! He himself was not feeling too well. The air smelt different for some reason, and his head was cold. Really, he just wanted to go to bed.

He addressed Security through the commchips.

'I'm turning in now,' he said. 'Y'all keep an eye out. Dr Ashanti connected up now? . . . Good, OK. Okey-doke.' Then he spoke to Auntie Auntie. 'Go on over to the lab and spend a little quality time with your boy Charlie,' he said. 'I ain't well. Just go on over and make them feel at home.'

On the way to the lab, Aneba passed Charlie a note he had written.

Dear Boy,

The others need a guide: the eagle could do it if you arrange it. Tonight, soon – please. Ship, northside, eat this note, love you.

Charlie read it and sniffed.

'What's that?' said Alex.

Charlie ate it. 'Medicine,' he said.

'All medicine should be approved by the Wellness Unit,' Alex said. 'Was that prescribed by the Wellness Unit?'

'Oh, I'm sorry, I didn't know,' said Charlie. 'I'll report it to them.' He smiled. The evening was darkening. 'Hang on a sec,' Charlie said. 'My shoe's undone.'

The others waited while he fell to his knees, a little off the path, out of the lighting. He took a long time and they ambled a little ahead, Aneba taking the lead.

'Wait, please,' said Alex.

'OK,' said Aneba.

Charlie meanwhile was whispering to Ninu, who he'd placed on his shoulder, hidden in the shadow of his collar. Ninu changed colour to match.

'So tell me about the island!' said Aneba. 'Isn't it beautiful! So many lovely plants!'

He started to crack jokes and laugh loudly. Alex and Sally-Ann were easily lured into a distracting conversation.

Ninu listened carefully, trying to pick up bird languages.

Nothing. Mostly they had gone home to roost.

There was one, though.

But it was Owl.

Why couldn't it be a lovely little hummingbird, or a chattery parrot?

'It's an owl,' whispered Ninu in Charlie's ear. Ninu was terrified of owls.

'Be brave,' whispered Charlie. 'I'm right here. Pretend you *are* an owl.'

Ninu took as deep a breath as his little body allowed, and called out.

'Did you hear that owl?' cried Sally-Ann, up ahead. 'It's really close!'

Ninu called again.

There was an answering hoot.

'Oh, there's another one!'

Aneba started into a long, noisy, amusing story about an owl who had once tried to sit on his head when he'd been riding a motorbike . . .

Ninu said, 'Brother Owl – the Catspeaking boy needs help. The humans who will rid the island of the bad humans need help. The Sweet Air is already clearing – they need help.'

'What help, Stranger Owl?' came the voice through the darkness.

'Go to the eagle on the highest peak,' said Ninu. 'Tell him there is a peculiar ship coming from the north bearing humans. Tell him to guide them safely to shore and direct them to the Animal Farm. Tell him this is life or death. This is life or death, Brother Owl.'

There was a silence.

Then a single hoot, and a low flap of wide wings passing in the darkness.

'He's doing it,' whispered Ninu.

Charlie stood up and called, 'All done! Sorry to keep you!'

Aneba closed his eyes in a moment of gratitude.

Charlie gave him a brilliant smile as he stepped back into the light. But he still wouldn't talk to him.

El Teflon was proceeding through the early evening, camouflaged, dim, soundless and undetected. As she approached the rocky northern shores of San Antonio, the crew became concerned that no guide had yet appeared.

'He'll be along,' said Magdalen grimly.

King Boris smiled in a confident fashion, to make everyone feel better.

Claudio skimmed the dark waters, looking, looking.

It was Elsina who spotted him.

'Whoo!' she called. 'Hey, look at *him*!'

That was when Magdalen saw him: swooping in, wingspan wide, head curled. It was the eagle.

And he saw the ship all right – eagles can see everything. He quartered the ship, bow to stern and then side

to side. And then again. Magdalen watched him, fascinated, and then nudged Claudio.

'I think that's our guide,' she murmured.

Claudio wasn't surprised. He'd been talked to by a chameleon in fluent Venetian dialect – nothing surprised him any more. He told King Boris, and King Boris alerted the captain.

'Are you sure?' said the captain. 'This is really not what we would expect . . .'

'Follow the bird,' King Boris said. 'This is out of our hands.'

Elsina and the Young Lion looked at each other. They were not convinced. They whispered to each other, and they came up with their own idea. As soon as they were within reach of land, they were going to head off alone. They could swim and follow a scent – what else did they need?

In the lab, Aneba set Alex and Sally-Ann to photocopying some diagrams. About 500 of them. They needed individual positioning on the photocopier, which happened to be at the other end of the room from the computer Charlie was using.

Charlie turned the computer on. Ninu sprawled himself carefully on top, turned his ear to the heart of the machine and listened. Aneba watched quietly.

'Charlie?' he said.

'Go away,' said Charlie.

Aneba, hideously aware of his commchip, and even more hideously aware of his son's anger, stepped back.

He found a scrap of paper and wrote on it: 'Do you know what you're doing?'

Charlie glanced at it, and glanced at Aneba. Then he took the piece of paper and scribbled: 'Do not spoil this. You must go away.'

Aneba read it. Then he wrote: 'The others are coming. Please come with me.'

Charlie glanced over. Ninu was still concentrating hard on the machine.

Charlie scribbled again: 'DAD! We'll come if we can, but leave me alone now.' Then he turned his back on his father, and Ninu began to whisper to him, and Charlie began to type, and Aneba stood back and watched in increasing amazement.

First Charlie logged on – as the HCE. He seemed to have all his passwords. Then he went into Security – again, he had the passwords. He logged on a second time, as the Security head. Step by step, with Ninu instructing him, typing swiftly and confidently, using each logon to confirm the order of the other, he began to disarm the entire system. He had learned with Brother Jerome how people with private police kept computer authority over all their employees and equipment – you needed to be able to disarm their weapons, for example, in case they mutinied. He hoped that the Corporacy was one of these distrusting employers.

All the while, Ninu whispered, and Charlie's heart pitter-pattered. With every keystroke he expected the machine to turn against him, discover him, freeze him out, blow up . . .

After four and a half minutes, he looked up. In theory, all doors and gates should now be unlocked, all cameras off, all weapons and response systems disarmed. Charlie watched the screen and waited. Had they got away with it?

Aneba stared. He desperately wanted to ask how his son was doing this – but he couldn't speak. He kind of croaked in frustrated amazement and Charlie shot him a furious look.

Then a text box flipped up on the blue screen. 'System self-damaging. Cannot self-damage. Default: ignore instruction to self-damage. Cannot continue.'

Charlie stared at it.

'Ninu?' he said.

'It's telling me the same thing,' he said, craning his head to listen carefully to the computer's inner language. 'It's saying . . . just that it can't dismantle itself.'

Charlie felt a hot and cold surge of blood under his skin. Of course their plan was risky. Of course there was no guarantee that it would work. But he couldn't believe that after they'd got this far . . .

What could he do? Security might be alerted at any moment, if the system was protecting itself.

OK. There was one thing at least that could help in the

long run. He went into email, and quickly rattled out a global message – one that would go to every address in the HCE's email addressbook. He added a few more, scraping addresses from his memory or making them up, hoping for the best: Brother Jerome, Prime Minister@UK, Dad's office in London, the Pope, the Dalai Lama, the Nelson Mandela Foundation, the United Nations, President of the Empire, the Venetian Revolutionary Government, King Boris . . .

THE CORPORACY IS ILLEGAL THE GHANA STARLETS ARE ON THEIR CARIBBEAN ISLAND SAN ANTONIO NEAR CUBA THEY KIDNAP PEOPLE AND ANIMALS COME AND HELP US PLEASE WE ARE TRYING TO ESCAPE ALSO SCIENTISTS AND CHILDREN PLEASE DO NOT LET THEM GET AWAY WITH IT AND THEY DRUG US AND FORCE US TO WORK FOR THEM SPECIALLY THE TALENTED PEOPLE PLEASE HELP US PLEASE

No time for anything better.

With a final keystroke, he sent it.

Well, it was a message in a bottle – who knew what results it would have?

For a moment he stopped to think. No one was here yet – what could he do? He focused his mind. Months ago, in Major Tib's cabin, he had listed among his strengths 'good at computers'. So how *did* they work? What was Ninu talking to that wouldn't dismantle itself? And was there something else that *could* dismantle it? Or destroy it? Crike, adults were always moaning about computers crashing, and losing things, and getting viruses . . .

'Ninu,' he whispered urgently. 'Listen for other voices, other languages. Maybe the operating system, or a dormant virus – ask if there's a virus protection we can take off . . .'

'A what?' said Ninu. He understood the computer's language, but that didn't mean he knew the subject. He didn't know what he was listening for.

Charlie bit his lip. They were really up against it now. How long did they have? No way of telling.

Ninu's eyes were riveted with concentration.

'Charlie!' he squeaked. 'Virus? There's something . . .' He was splayed flat on the box, absorbing information through his whole self. 'There's a virus – says he wants to come in – he's in . . . cyberspace? Something about a portal . . . Horton?'

Basic anti-virus software, thought Charlie. I can find that.

He really, really wished he had an hour or so to do this properly. Any wrong move and the thing might freeze or lock him out. His fingers flickered over the keyboard . . .

Portal protection virus-scope! That looked right. Well, now or never.

He clicked *Uninstall*.

Breathed calmly and carefully. Waited for the icons to disappear.

Pop!

Gone.

OK.

Come on, broadband maximus, do your stuff. Ride those little viruses in, shift that global email out . . .

That was when twelve large and muscular armed securityguys burst into the lab.

'Hold it right there!' shouted the leader. 'What's going on here?'

'Research, of course,' said Aneba. 'Really – what are you thinking of? The HCE specifically told me – promised me – that we would not be disturbed in our work, and here we are on our very first night and you're bursting in like some secret police waving your guns . . .'

They did have guns.

The screen was still blank.

'Step away from the computer terminal,' said the leader. 'We are informed that inappropriate programming activity resulting in a security alert has been activated at this terminal.'

'Who by?' asked Charlie.

It was at this point that Auntie Auntie turned up, a swift bustle of glamour stepping into the lab, coming, she thought, to have a quiet look at the new arrivals on their first evening.

'What is all this?' she cried out. 'What is going on here?'

'Inappropriate activity,' repeated the leader. 'Step against the wall, please,' he said to Charlie.

'What inappropriate activity?' asked Auntie Auntie. 'What are you doing to this child?'

'Against the wall?' said Aneba. 'Why? What's going on?' His question was as much to Charlie, who had one eye on the guards and one on the screen.

'Sorry, madame, sorry,' said the leader to Auntie Auntie. He was cradling his gun. 'Step away, son.' His voice carried a tinge more threat.

'OK, sorry,' said Charlie, with his big innocent grin. 'No problemo.' His heart was pounding. What, if anything, had he managed to achieve? Would the mail get through? Were the systems down?

Looking at the gun on the arm of the man in front of him, he realized that the problem was more immediate. If the weapons were computerized, and he'd managed to disarm them, OK. If they weren't, or he hadn't . . . well, he'd better think of something quick.

The leader nodded to another man who had come in behind them.

'Clear to check now, sir,' he said, covering Aneba and Charlie. Alex and Sally-Ann had come up from the other end.

'What *is* this?' asked Sally-Ann.

'Inappropriate activity,' said the leader again, as if that answered everything.

'What garbage,' said Sally-Ann. 'They're doing their jobs, what they were brought here for . . .'

The securityguy stared at her in surprise. For a moment everybody stood, suspended, uncertain . . . and then Sally-Ann started to have hysterics.

'Brought here!' she yelled. 'Brought here! What are any of us doing here? What are you doing? What's happening to us, what's happening?!!!' She flung her arms out, knocking over a flask, which fell on to a screen, which fizzled and started to smoke.

Charlie seized the opportunity. Chaos – that's what he needed. He shoved with his elbow and knocked over a metal stand, which fell against the window with a big rackety crash. With his foot, at the same time, he kicked a plug and turned some lights out.

And chaos he got.

At that moment, Sergei, who had been keeping lookout, mraowled loudly, and Charlie, looking up, saw behind the securityguys a stream of furious, brilliant, joyful FREE animals. Fantastic! It had worked! The gates had opened, and the animals were coming to *his* rescue! At their head was a fine-looking leopard, and two Lions, who appeared to be sopping wet . . . Charlie looked again. He'd seen no big cats at the Animal Farm . . . Could it . . . Elsina? The Young Lion? He was gobsmacked. What were they doing here? But there was no time – the securityguys stopped, turned round and froze.

Oh no, thought Charlie. They're going to shoot them all. They're going to kill them. But they didn't. Whatever they were trained for, they were for this moment too amazed to know what to do.

It was happening so quickly. Elsina and the Young Lion showed their teeth, bunched up their shoulders and within moments the securityguys were huddled into a group, surrounded by twitching tails. Then the Lions just stood staring at them, their teeth showing and their jaws dripping. The leopard joined them. They looked quite terrifying. Every now and then one of them growled and roared. The securityguys seemed to be in shock.

A crowd of cats and dogs had positioned themselves with the Lions, baring their teeth and growling. The cats had come to a halt and were staring, hissing, some of them sheathing and unsheathing their claws. They covered the floor, the tables and desks, the machinery. There were an awful lot of them.

'Hey, Charlie!' cried the Young Lion.

'Hey, Charlie!' giggled Elsina.

Charlie called back to them, a cat-cry of love and joy.

But it broke the spell. In a single movement the leader turned his gun and shot Elsina. The sound released the other men from their trance. The guards started shooting into the animal throng. The noise was dreadful, shattering. Charlie gasped and threw his hands up.

'No, no, no!' he shouted. 'Elsina!' He shouted her name in Cat, a visceral shriek from the depths of him, from his cat self. It was a fearsome howl.

And then a horrible silence. Everything was wrong.

And then a cat began to laugh.

Nothing had happened. The animals were all fine. No blood, no howling or moaning, no falling over.

The dogs were still growling, the cats were still keening. It was securityguys who began to moan and shout, their weapons falling from their hands, the teeth and claws of the animals they had thought they were killing surrounding them, bared and drooling . . .

It had worked! He had disarmed the weapons!

Charlie gave a yell of triumph.

'Your weapons are useless, big boy!' he cried. 'You've been disarmed. All systems down, all change, out with the old, in with the new. Go and breathe some fresh air and relax. The Corporacy is over!'

'Charlie?' said Auntie Auntie, but he didn't listen to her. He was running to the Lions, and hugging them, and hugging them, and hugging them.

'Everything is changing now, madame,' said Aneba softly. 'You might want to change too.'

Auntie Auntie stared at him.

The securityguys stared at Charlie. What was he talking about? And what was he *doing*?

'Wow,' said Sally-Ann. She was as white as a sheet and her eyes were shining.

'Wow,' said Alex.

The leader shouted, 'Reinforcements! Reinforcements at lab twelve!'

Charlie snorted. He hadn't managed to close down the commchip circuit. More securityguys would come, and then what? He yelled a word to the Young Lion, who leapt on the leader and pinned him to the floor. The man shut up, and across the island the rest of security heard through their commchips only a heavy panting sound.

Meanwhile something peculiar was going on. Aneba was on his knees before Elsina.

'Please,' he said. It took a moment for her to understand – he was stripping off the dressing that covered the wound on his neck, and gesturing. She saw the lump.

'Charlie, tell her!' Aneba called out.

Charlie smiled, and explained swiftly. Elsina was a little surprised, but she understood, and delicately, with one elegant claw, she swiped Aneba's wound open. Aneba ripped out the chip, grinned, and slapped the dressing back on. Stitches could come later – but at least now he was free to talk and listen.

Suddenly a voice from behind stopped him.

'Me too!' cried Sally-Ann. 'Me too! Come on, Alex!'

Alex paused for a moment, then fell on his knees too and bared his neck.

'Any more?' cried Charlie. 'Any more for a free future? Any more individuals here who'd like to lead their own life? Come on down, come on down, ladies and gentlemen – come on, Auntie, give it a go . . .' He felt the spirit of Major Tib in him, crying out like a circus barker.

'Different claw for each person, Elsina!' Charlie said. 'We don't want any diseases spreading.' He grabbed some disinfectant (labs are handy for supplies) and poured it over her paw.

Sally-Ann gasped at the pain as Elsina slit the scar over her commchip with a sharp swipe. Like Aneba, she found the thing herself and tore it out.

'Good riddance!' she whooped, throwing it across the room.

One of the soldiers at the back pushed his way forward.

'Please,' he said. 'Take mine out.'

'YES!' cried Charlie. 'That's what we want. Well done, lad! Any more for any more? Come on now, you've been breathing free air for a day, any more of you tough enough to do it? You, sir, you know you want to . . .' He singled out the leader, still prone beneath the Young Lion. The leader shrank away.

'I'll do it for you,' said the Young Lion with a dangerous grin, and lifted his sharp curved claws.

The man winced. 'Reinforcements,' he whispered in a hollow voice.

The Young Lion, in a single elegant movement, nicked the guard's neck. 'You'll thank me for it,' he purred softly, but, of course, the guard knew nothing of that. He just fainted.

Another of his men was coming down to Elsina.

Charlie cheered, and passed out disinfectant and wads of gauze for people to staunch the blood.

Elsina was as careful as she could be. She didn't want to pierce any jugular veins by mistake.

Aneba put his hand gently on Auntie Auntie's shoulder. 'Go on, sister,' he whispered to her in Twi.

She gave him a quick, terrified look.

'God didn't give you a brain just for you to let somebody else run it,' he said, and he smiled.

Auntie Auntie fell to her knees with the others.

The reinforcements, when they arrived, took one look at the queue on their knees and joined it. They had, after all, been trained to do the same thing as everybody else.

The Young Lion said, 'I'll give you a hand, shall I?'

'You'd better,' said Elsina. 'I've only enough clean claws for ten.'

'I'll help as well, then, shall I?' said the leopard.

Only he said it in English. Clear, beautiful English, with a definite Ghanaian accent.

Charlie's head snapped round.

The leopard looked up and smiled at him through his whiskers.

'Hello again,' he said. In English.

Auntie Auntie fainted.

Sally-Ann gasped.

Aneba stopped stock-still.

The securityguys didn't hear it – they couldn't believe it and it passed over their heads.

But Charlie – Charlie looked the leopard in the eye, and

he smiled, and he said, 'Well, hello again to you too.' He approached the leopard, who he hadn't seen since he was a baby in that Ghanaian forest, and he held out his hand. Then he changed his mind, and he laid his cheek against the leopard's cheek, and there were tears in his eyes.

One after another, all around them, the Corporacy people laid their heads down before the Lions and bared their necks for liberation.

CHAPTER

EIGHTEEN

'Sir,' whispered the HCE's valet, 'something is going on. You may want to wake up.'

By the time he reached the lab, there was nothing there but a bunch of shattered-looking people holding gauze to their necks and wondering where they could get a cup of tea. One enterprising group was preparing to lead them all to the dining room, to make some.

'You should have tea in your rooms at this time!' cried the HCE. 'What's going on? What's –?'

He stopped. He had just realized the significance of the neck wounds.

'Hi, Paul,' said one of the securityguys.

Paul? Nobody here called him Paul. He wasn't called Paul any more. Nobody had called him Paul since . . .

He felt dreadful.

'What's going on?' he asked. It came out slightly pathetic.

But nobody stopped to listen. They wanted their tea. 'Come on,' said Sally-Ann. 'I know where the biscuits are.' She took him by the arm and led him out into the corridor.

The children were all awake, waiting to hear from Charlie about their escape. They were lurking in the undergrowth round the schoolhouses. They'd noticed that the doors were all open – even the door to the tunnel to the mountain.

And they noticed all right when the animals started to pour out of the door. A stream of cats and dogs, Sphynx kittens and Allergenies, lizards and – 'Oh my, it's a leopard!' shrieked Seventeen.

The leopard smiled at her and said very gallantly, 'True, my dear – my name is George.'

Seventeen shrieked again and Twenty-One sat down rather suddenly and said, 'Ohmygodsweetlordjesusinheaven.'

The Starlets stared.

The other animals of the island shifted in their nests and burrows. What was all this racket? The night animals came to look.

'Whoo whoo!' cried the owl.

'Crikey O'Reilly!' screeched the crickets.

'Lordamercy,' called the nightingales. The farm animals were out!

And there was Charlie – striding between two Lions, with a chameleon on his shoulder, a cat at his feet and an eagle whispering in his ear! (In fact, it was whispering to Ninu, who was telling him to tell the people on *El Teflon* to stop trying to find a landing spot on the north coast and come straight here to the beach.)

The children gaped.

The eagle swooped across the night sky, back to Fidel's ship.

On the beach was magnificent chaos. Sally-Ann was throwing open the stores by the dining room, and all the animals and humans were helping themselves and one another in a fabulous free-for-all feast.

Charlie sat with his friends on a rock facing the sea. The moon was rising, huge and yellow.

Aneba came up to him.

'Charlie?'

In his joy and relief, Charlie had forgotten that he was angry with his father.

'Charlie, how did you do it?' Aneba asked. He was looking at his son with something like awe.

'I used my intelligence, Dad,' he said. 'Like you taught me.'

'But how . . .?'

'Ninu translated,' Charlie said. 'He got the computer language, the programming, off the computer, and had the computer tell me what to do.'

Aneba began to laugh. 'Oh my word, my word,' he said. 'My clever boy. How did you know?'

'I didn't,' said Charlie. 'I wondered, and we checked, and then we took a punt.'

They both remembered when he had used that word before. He didn't use it on purpose now to make his father feel bad – it just slipped out.

Aneba accepted it. 'Charlie,' he said. 'I'm sorry. I really didn't think it was possible.'

'You should have listened to me, Dad,' said Charlie. 'I'd have explained, if you'd listened.'

'Sorry,' said Aneba.

Charlie stared at him.

'Dad,' he said. 'You know Rafi . . .'

'Yeah, where is he, that little –'

'No, Dad. Wait.' This was going to be hard. 'Dad. You know Mabel.'

'Of course I know Mabel. What are you talking about?'

How could he put it?

'Mabel's his mum.'

Bluntly, evidently.

'What?'

It was good that Aneba had just made a fool of himself not believing and trusting Charlie, because otherwise he would have done it again.

'Mabel told me about her kid, and it being adopted, and the new mum's name was Martha Sortch.'

'Martha Sortch.'

'Yeah.'

'That's Rafi's mum's name.'

'Yeah.'

For a moment Aneba's face was unreadable, and then he broke into his biggest grin.

'Well, where is he?' Aneba roared. 'Come on, Charlie, he's family! That's Mabel's boy – where is he? Is he all right?'

Charlie took a step back. Family? Mabel's boy?

'Er, Dad . . .' he said.

'Yes, Charlie, I know. Mabel should have been more careful and he has fallen in with a bad crowd. All the more reason why his family should rally round him now . . .'

Charlie's jaw dropped. His dad was really the most extraordinary man.

Behind Aneba, under the rising Caribbean moon, streams of animals flowed out into the warm night, followed by bunches of Corporacy staff clutching wads of gauze to their necks. More Corporacy staff were coming out from their bedrooms, confused and alarmed, their commchips going crazy with animal noises, security not responding, their doors hanging open, their heads feeling chilly and their thoughts wayward. The HCE was standing in the middle of it all, eating a custard cream.

I did this, Charlie thought.

Aneba turned round to join his son's survey of the scene. 'Perhaps you should make a speech,' he murmured.

But there was no chance, because at that moment a sound was heard in the distance – a musical sound, wild and sweet, swirling and cheerful, a rhythmic, funny sound, all oompah and tarantella . . . The wakening animals heard it and peered from their nests and burrows. The people heard it and turned to one another, saying, 'What *is* that?' as if they half recognized it (which they did). The Lions' eyes opened wide, and Charlie turned to Aneba and yelled, 'Dad! Dad! It's the Calliope!'

'The what?' said Aneba as the noise drew nearer and louder.

'It's the *Circe*!' Charlie yelled, beginning to hop up and down. 'What's she doing here? Oh, fantastic! Fantastic! Dad, it's the Circus I ran away with! And Dad! Mabel will be on board!'

Aneba narrowed his eyes.

And then Charlie stopped hopping up and down – because it was the Circus the Lions ran away *from*, with his help . . . but he couldn't really believe any bad thing could happen now. Nevertheless, he rushed to the Lions.

'It's the *Circe*,' hissed the Young Lion.

'I know,' said Charlie. 'Do you want to hide?'

'No, I blooming don't,' said the Young Lion. 'I want to find that blooming Maccomo and bite his head off . . .'

Charlie realized he had no idea where Maccomo was – or Rafi. He'd been so busy bringing down the Corporacy that he'd – well, he couldn't do everything.

'There are more ships!' cried Aneba, peering into the darkness and trying to make out from the lights how many there were.

Within moments it was apparent: there on the beach

Calliope's Grand Finale

R. LOCKHART

were Magdalen (hugging Charlie), Claudio (mightily relieved to see the Lions), King Boris, Major Tib, Mabel, Pirouette, Hans, Julius, Sara and Tara, a brigade of Lucidis including Sigi, El Diablo Aero, the Hungarian with the Performing Bees, Mr Andrews . . . they were all staring at the chaotic scene in front of them.

'Turn the darn Calliope off!' shouted Major Tib. 'What in heck is going on here? Mabel! Thought ya said there was an extra gig for us before the tour starts up . . . What in heck?'

He had seen Charlie.

'Hey, Major Tib!' cried Charlie. 'Did you meet my mum and dad? Mum is Mabel's sister!'

'YOU!' roared Major Tib. 'What nonsense you talkin', boy? Where's my darn Lions and where's that nogoodnik Maccomo? What's been going on and why y'all here?'

'I'll tell you everything,' said Charlie. 'When I've got a moment!'

But then he caught sight of Julius, and had to go and punch him on the shoulder in a manly greeting (they were extremely pleased to see each other again), and then the monkeys peering from the palms noticed the monkeys who had crept into the *Circe*'s rigging, and then, of course, all hell broke loose.

First the monkeys started yelling to one another, and then Mabel's tigers started yelling at them to shut up, and then Elsina and the Young Lion started yelling to the tigers, and the leopard joined in, and then the zebras got nervous and started neighing and prancing in their stablecabins, so Blue the web-footed dog barked at them to calm them down, and the Hungarian's bees noticed the hummingbirds (who couldn't possibly sleep through all this racket) and started to swarm, and Claudio and Sigi Lucidi were chatting in Italian, and Magdalen was trying to fight her way through the crowd to Mabel, who was staring in horror at the figure of Maccomo, in his nightshirt, emerging out of the forest with a look on his face like a frozen ghost, while unnoticed in the corner Rafi was standing with the other field hands, smoking a pickpocketed cigarette and staring in disbelief. Unnoticed, that is, except by Aneba, who was striding towards him with a manly look in his eye.

Oh, and nobody had stopped the Calliope.

'Pretty good mess, in'it?' murmured Sergei.

'Fantastic,' said Charlie, grinning, one hand on the Young Lion's head and one on Elsina's.

'I'm glad I'm in your pocket, though,' said Ninu.

POSTSCRIPT

Many curious conversations were had that night, but only one needs reporting.

Aneba did not immediately tell Rafi of his change in family status. Instead he collared him, and brought him – well, frogmarched him – to where Mabel and Magdalen were embracing Charlie. Major Tib was there as well, and Aneba did not require him to leave.

Rafi had struggled a bit, so Aneba held him in a half nelson for the duration. This meant he was addressing the back of his head.

Magdalen, when she saw them coming, told Aneba to hand him over to Fidel's men, so they could put him on the secure gunship with the HCE and Maccomo.

'Wait,' said Aneba. 'Rafi, stop wriggling.'

Rafi kicked Aneba's shin.

'Oh, behave,' said Aneba. He grabbed Rafi into a full nelson – both arms pinned behind his back – and turned him round to face Mabel.

'Sister,' he said. 'I am sorry not to be able to do this

with more ceremony, but I'm afraid this is your son.'

Magdalen said, 'No it's not, it's Rafi Sadler, you dork.'

'Rafi Sadler, adopted son of Martha Sortch,' said Aneba. 'Aged seventeen. When's your birthday, Rafi?'

Rafi had stopped wriggling. 'I don't know,' he said. 'Martha made one up for me. Said my real one didn't matter.'

Mabel was staring at him.

'You?' she said softly.

Rafi stared brazenly back. 'Yeah. Me,' he said insolently. 'So?' He hadn't shaved for days, and in his boyish stubble there was a shadow of russet.

'Manners!' said Aneba firmly, giving him a little shake.

'Yeah, well, I wasn't brought up right, was I?' sneered Rafi. He was staring right at Mabel and the look in his eye was almost hatred.

'True,' said Aneba. 'Which is what we now need to address. Mabel?'

'I'm your mum,' she whispered.

'So what, you're going to be my mum, then, are you? Make up for dumping me? Are you?'

'Yes,' she whispered.

Rafi glared defiantly at her. 'Yeah, right,' he said. And then he burst into tears. He turned round and wept on Aneba's broad chest. Then he flung himself at his mother and wept on her red hair. Then he got extremely embarrassed.

'It's all right,' Charlie heard himself saying.

'No, it's sniking not!' yelled Rafi. 'I'm a complete gras-pole and I always will be and I don't deserve a family . . .'

'Shut up,' said Mabel softly, and took him back in her arms. 'We can work it out.' She glanced up at Magdalen and Aneba. 'Can't we?'

'Um, yes,' said Magdalen. 'Won't be easy, but –'

'Of course we can!' shouted Aneba. 'He's family! This is our nephew! Charlie's cousin!'

Charlie stared at his cousin. Yeah, right. That was going to be fun. Not. Or . . . Well . . . Oh dear.

In the end, around about dawn, everybody went to bed. Charlie slept with two Lions, one leopard, Hans, Julius, several cats and a chameleon. The dogs moved in with the Starlets, to whom they had taken a fancy, and Seventeen and Twenty-One adopted the Jesus Lizard, Pirouette and Auntie Auntie, who was still in a state of shock.

Magdalen and Aneba sat up late with Major Tib and Mabel (once Magdalen could be prised from her son's side, and persuaded that he was OK with the Lions to guard him, and Mabel could be prised from hers).

No one could decide what to do with Rafi, because although he was the long-lost child, he was also pretty high up in the villain department, and while they didn't want to mistrust him right at the beginning of the new family life, they actually, well, didn't trust him. In the end Aneba said he'd just keep him in the half nelson all night, and see how things went.

The HCE and Maccomo spent the night on a Cuban gunship, where it was felt they wouldn't make any trouble.

The next day, after a late breakfast, Charlie convened a huge meeting, at which everybody – animals included – was to say what they wanted to do now. Ninu and Charlie would translate.

It was a complete shambles, of course, because mostly people wanted to turn back time, and go and live with their parents in their happy childhood days, but that wasn't exactly possible, so Charlie moved them on swiftly to real things that they wanted. It ended up, after an awful lot of hooing and haing, like this:

1. Elsina and the Young Lion wanted to go home, and take Charlie with them, and Maccomo too so that they could keep him prisoner properly this time.
2. Major Tib wanted Elsina and the Young Lion to rejoin the Circus, and George the leopard too, and Charlie if he promised not to steal any more animals.
3. Magdalen wanted to go home to London and have a long hot bath.
4. Aneba wanted to collect samples of all the plants on the island before going home to London and having a long hot bath.
5. Mabel wanted to stay with the Circus, and to take Rafi too, and to teach him all she knew.

6. Sergei wanted to go wherever Charlie was going.

7. Ninu wanted to go wherever Charlie was going, as long as that was back to Essaouira.

8. Claudio wanted to go back to Venice with King Boris.

9. King Boris wanted to deliver the HCE to Interpol, because, as he said, all this is all very well but there is such a thing as the rule of law.

10. Jungko the fork-tailed cat wanted to join the Circus, if Marta the nesting cat was allowed to come too, though she couldn't quite see how they would make a performance, but she promised they would try.

11. Marta the nesting cat wanted to go wherever Jungko was going.

12. Seventeen and Twenty-One wanted to go home to Ghana and find their mother.

13. Auntie Auntie wanted a strong brandy, and then, she supposed, perhaps a fabulous job in New York.

14. George actually quite wanted to join the Circus too, but he was embarrassed to admit it.

15. The tigers wanted to stay with Mabel; in fact, one of them nearly cried just at the idea of going anywhere without her.

16. The wild monkeys wanted the circus monkeys to come and join them on the island.

17. The circus monkeys wanted to join the wild monkeys on the island.

18. The zebras also wanted to join the wild monkeys on the island.

19. The bees had flown away.

20. Julius wanted himself and Hans and Charlie to stay on the island and found a children's and animals' Free Republic.

21. Hans wanted to bring the Learned Pig along with him.

22. The Learned Pig wanted to stop being Learned, if that was all right, as it wasn't really his nature, and could he just stay on the beach?

23. Blue wanted to stay with Jake Yeboa, wherever he was going.

24. Jake Yeboa wanted to go home and train for the World Cup, and win it.

25. The other Starlets wanted to do what Jake Yeboa wanted, and could they take the dogs with them too?

26. The HCE wanted everybody to listen to reason, so that things could get back to normal, but . . . well, he was shouted down.

27. Maccomo wouldn't say what he wanted. When pressed, he said he wanted Mabel. When she said, 'Not on your nelly, slaver,' he said – to Charlie's surprise – that the animals should get whatever they wanted and the humans should rot, because humans caused all the damage in the world and the sooner

they made themselves extinct, the better it would
be for all the other creatures.

28. Rafi wanted to go back to Europe. He'd work his
passage, he said. Maybe on the *Circe*, if they'd have
him. He'd hang out with Mabel if she wanted, he
supposed. He wanted to find his dog, he said, who
he'd lost touch with in Paris.

29. Sally-Ann wanted to make everybody some more
food. And then go home. She was from Tennessee.
She thought. Somewhere in Tennessee.

30. Alex didn't know what he wanted, but he'd think
about it.

31. Pirouette wanted not to miss the beginning of the
Mississippi tour, because she had been perfecting a
rather extraordinary new flying trapeze move.

32. Madame Barbue, the Bearded Lady, said she wanted
to set up a sweet shop in Paris, and, actually, since
you asked, not be bearded any more. At that Auntie
Auntie woke up and said, 'Well, that's easy,' and
went off to make her a potion.

And Charlie?

Well, first Charlie wanted a good long uninterrupted
session on the computer with Ninu, dismantling all the
Corporacy Communities and following up his worldwide
alert. He'd do that after lunch. In the meantime, he arranged
that he, his mum, his dad, Sergei, Ninu and everybody who

wanted to join the Circus would do so, until the Circus reached their hometown (as it was bound to in due course), whereupon they would be free to go home if they wanted – as he would. The Lions, the Starlets (and the dogs), and Seventeen and Twenty-One would all go home with Younus, who would stop off in Ghana on the way to Essaouira. No humans would stay on San Antonio: the animals would take it over, and the humans who did not want to accept a ride with Younus or the *Circe* could all go to Cuba with the warships and think things through from there. Unless they wanted to go to Haiti.

So in a way everybody got what they wanted except:

1. Julius, who had to forsake his idea of a Free Republic.
2. Major Tib, but he had the tigers and now George, and the two peculiar new cats took up no room, and Mabel would be glad to have her sister, and the husband looked good at least, he could do some strongman thing, no doubt . . . so Major Tib was happy enough. At least Mabel hadn't said she wanted to leave. Major Tib suddenly realized that, actually, he wanted to marry Mabel. But when he tried to bring it up, Mabel gave such a horrified look that Charlie and the Lions got the giggles, so that was that.
3. Charlie, who didn't tell anyone that 49.9 per cent of him wanted to go and be with the Lions in the forest.

(Elsina and the Young Lion knew, but they'd already made their peace, and said their goodbyes.)

4. Alex, who, not knowing what he wanted, was fated never to achieve it.

5. The HCE, who didn't deserve it anyway.

6. Maccomo, who to make things easier, was offered the choice of going to Interpol with King Boris and the HCE, or going back with the Lions. He chose the Lions.

7. Ninu, who had to choose between Charlie and home.

He chose Charlie, of course.

The End . . . forever.

TO NEW ORLEANS

THE CARIBBEAN

SAN ANTONIO

The flotilla

Fidel's place

CUBA

JAMAICA

N

SCALE: from here to here = NOT THAT FAR

OLD YELLER
(Maccomo, Charlie & Rafi)

SULEIMAN'S JOY
(Magdalen & Aneba)

San Antonio & Neighbouring Islands

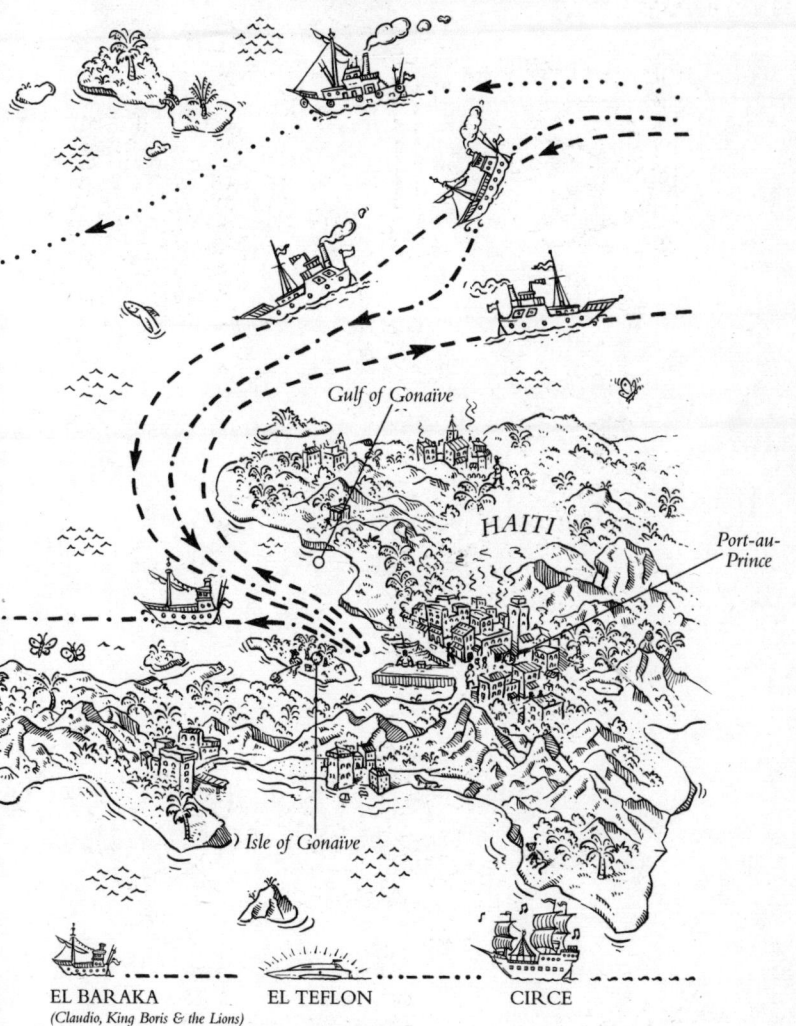

Gulf of Gonaïve

HAITI

Port-au-Prince

Isle of Gonaïve

EL BARAKA
(Claudio, King Boris & the Lions)

EL TEFLON

CIRCE